Praise for Jess Dee's
Office Affair

"*Office Affair* is yet another HOT book by Jess Dee!! She once again grabs you from beginning to end with a great story of how two people deal with the hurts and failures of the past."

~ *Guilty Pleasures Book Reviews*

"WOW is all I have to say for Jess Dee's *Office Affair*. Right from the start I was hooked, and boy, once you start reading the latest from her, you're not going to want to put it down... This is definitely a book that will rock your senses."

~ *Fallen Angel Reviews*

"*Office Affair* is a must read if you are looking for an emotional, highly sexual, journey of two career driven people. I highly recommend *Office Affair*. The writing just sucks you, takes you on an emotional journey, spiced up with hot encounters, and then slowly lets you back down."

~ *Sizzling Hot Book Reviews*

"*Office Affair* is the whole ball of wax—witty, sensual, humorous and packed full of sexy suspense... Bravo Ms. Dee— you've got another erotic masterpiece on your hands!"

~ *TwoLips Reviews*

Look for these titles by
Jess Dee

Now Available:

Office Affair

Jess Dee

SAMHAIN
PUBLISHING

Samhain Publishing, Ltd.
11821 Mason Montgomery Road, 4B
Cincinnati, OH 45249
www.samhainpublishing.com

Office Affair
Copyright © 2013 by Jess Dee
Print ISBN: 978-1-61921-116-2
Digital ISBN: 978-1-60928-927-0

Editing by Jennifer Miller
Cover by Angela Waters

First Samhain Publishing, Ltd. electronic publication: May 2012
First Samhain Publishing, Ltd. print publication: April 2013

Dedication

Kitty Kelly, this one's for you. Because you asked for it, and because without you, the book would not exist.

And as always—thank you, Jennifer. This time, you deserve an extra special thank you. If these edits didn't defeat you, nothing will!

Chapter One

"You want to know what I think?"

Ben Cowley jerked his head up at the unexpected voice. He'd been so immersed in figures, he'd had no idea anyone was in his office. Hell, he'd had no idea anyone was left in the building. At this time of night he'd assumed everyone else had gone home.

"I always want to know what you think." He flashed the woman standing in the doorway his biggest smile, knowing his flirting was shameless.

"I think you need to get laid. And you need to get laid soon."

The smile vanished. "Pardon?"

"You're a mess, Ben. You have been since you transferred to the Sydney office."

A muscle twitched in his jaw, but he tried not to show any other emotion—even though his stomach clenched in a nasty knot. Ben raised an eyebrow in question. "Is there a reason we're having this conversation?"

She gave him a somber nod. "You've changed. You're not the same person you were when we first met. It's almost as if you've lost your enthusiasm, lost your drive. People are starting to talk—"

"People?"

"Well, me," she admitted sheepishly. "And maybe not quite talk. It's more like I'm getting worried about you."

Ben looked wryly at her. She cut an imposing figure. Tall—made even taller by the four-inch heels she always wore—slim and dressed to kill in her high-powered business suit. Melissa Sparks was a no-nonsense, one-hundred-percent goal-oriented investment banker. Much like Ben was.

She took her work seriously, clocking up even longer hours than Ben used to. She was known to be top of her field, and working with her—learning from her—made Ben a better banker.

But damn, when the woman smiled, light filled the office. Lately Ben had made it his life's purpose to get her to smile, and he wasn't above using any means possible, which included shameless flirting at any opportunity.

Flirting with Melissa was safe. She'd been careful to delineate the boundaries of their relationship from day one, when he'd still lived in Newcastle. They were colleagues, end of story. If Ben had a business-related issue or problem, he could always rely on her to help him solve it. Ben had spent enough time in the Sydney office over the eighteen months prior to moving there to have developed a deep respect for her business acumen.

"It's not like you to worry, Melissa."

She wrinkled her nose as she regarded him. "Look, may I be frank?"

Ben snorted. "You haven't been so far?"

She ignored his sarcasm. "You need a woman. Someone to look after you, to worry about you, to send meals into work so when you forget to buy lunch like you always do, you don't starve. Someone who'll care for your emotional side so you can focus on business. You need someone tender and loving in your life. Someone like Sienna."

Ben gave her a hard stare. "Sienna and I are over. You

know that."

"Of course I know that," she said. "If I didn't, I wouldn't be here talking about this. Thing is, you've changed. You're not the same man you were before you moved here."

Ben gritted his teeth, trying not to respond. Melissa was correct. He was different. There was very little left of the Ben who'd had his heart so thoroughly destroyed.

"You're...harder. Angrier. And more tense than I've ever seen you." As she spoke, Melissa did something Ben hadn't seen her do in the more than two years he'd known her. She rummaged her fingers through her hair, loosening the severe ponytail she wore most every day. She must have removed several clips and an elastic, because when she dropped her hands, a mane of hair tumbled over her shoulders and fell halfway down her back in a wild mess of russet tresses.

He forced himself not to gape. Sure, he knew Melissa had long hair. Even when it was tied up, she couldn't hide its length. What he'd never dreamed was how long it was, or how thick. Or how much it transformed her face when it hung loose, softening her features. With hair flowing down around her neck and shoulders, her hazel eyes looked more relaxed—more sensuous, even, and her small, pointy nose looked not quite so pointy. Not pointy at all. As for her lips...

Well, hell.

Her lips were luscious, pouty and downright kissable. Ben had to take another look, wondering if she'd applied a subtle shade of gloss or lipstick before she'd walked into his office.

"Harder, angrier and more tense?" he repeated, forcing himself to focus on Melissa's words and not on her unexpected beauty.

"Do you disagree?"

Ben frowned. It was impossible to disagree. Since Sienna

11

had left him he'd been forced to steel himself against his own heart. Forced to build walls around his emotions so he wouldn't have to think about the bone-deep agony that had almost crushed him after their relationship ended. Those walls had helped him ignore the humiliation of losing Sienna to another man. They'd also helped him ignore the ways he'd changed and the fact that he didn't particularly like those changes.

But the measures he'd taken to protect himself had been private ones. He'd never intended for others to see the changes and the heartbreak he'd undergone. Apparently, Melissa hadn't missed a damn thing. "Is that really how you see me?"

Sympathy softened her gaze. "I never used to. You were always the happiest person I knew. Content with your career and happy at home. You laughed all the time. Now you only seem to laugh when you remember it's necessary."

"Well, hell." Ben ran a weary hand over his face.

"My thoughts exactly. Which brings me back to what I said when I first stepped into your office. You need to get laid."

"You don't mince words, do you?"

"If I minced words, I wouldn't be earning the kind of money I am."

She earned good money. Ben would know, since he earned a similar income. Less than her, though, because for the last year or so, he'd cut back his hours. "So, you think it's that simple? I get laid, and I lose the edge." He grinned humorlessly. "A little sex and I'll be the same happy Ben I used to be."

He'd tried that. Often. It hadn't made him happy.

"No, I think it's far more complex than that, and perceiving sex as a cure-all for a broken heart is an inadequate method of getting over her. But it would be a start. A step in the right direction. Tell me, Ben. Have you slept with anyone besides Sienna in the last year?"

Ben's spine stiffened. "Be careful, Melissa. You're crossing a line you have no place crossing."

Even though she had no business asking, Ben couldn't help but wonder why the question worried him. Was it too personal an area of his life for a colleague to probe into? Or was he being overly defensive, because for the last few months he'd found himself having sex altogether too often? In altogether too...unusual circumstances?

"I know I am." She busied herself opening the two buttons of her jacket, slipping it off and slinging it over her shoulder.

For the second time in one evening, Ben had to force himself not to gape. Melissa never removed her jacket. Not even on the hottest, most humid summer days.

The shirt she had on was just as professional as the suit she wore, a sensible, button-up white blouse. It showed no cleavage but could not hide the swell of her breasts. The woman had hidden a handful more than Ben would have guessed.

Not that he'd given much thought to Melissa's breasts before. Her businesslike attitude and the jackets she wore covered her womanly bits too well for his mind to ever wander off in that direction. But the way she'd positioned her arm now, with her hand resting on her shoulder holding the jacket and her elbow sticking out, her breast was pushed forward, catching Ben's attention.

He drew his gaze away. "If you know that, why are you even asking?"

"Because I miss the Ben you used to be. I want him back. Working with you was always more fun when you were happy."

They'd worked together often over the last two-odd years. Even when he'd lived in Newcastle, Ben had spent long hours in the Sydney head office, most of the time with Melissa, finalizing deals and working out investments and bonds.

Ben couldn't help but be struck by Melissa's honesty. He liked that she'd thought of him as fun once. He'd always seen himself as focused and determined. Too much of both perhaps.

"You were also far more productive and creative back then," Melissa said. "Did you know you've signed twenty-five percent fewer deals in the first six months of this year than you did in the same time last year?"

"Perhaps that's because I cut back my hours by twenty-five percent this year." For Sienna's sake. She'd left him because he'd worked too hard and spent too much time at the office, so he'd attempted to rectify the problem. Not that it had helped.

"It's not only that." Melissa shook her head, sending those wild tresses tumbling all over the place. "Your heart's just not in your work anymore. I'm not seeing that desire to succeed, that drive to be the best. It used to be so much a part of you."

Never mind work, the sad truth was his heart wasn't *anywhere* anymore. It wasn't in his job—although the work still stimulated him to no end—and it wasn't safe in Sienna's hands. It was lost. And that loss hurt him. A lot. More than he was willing to confess.

Ben sighed. "Look, Melissa, I'm sorry. I'm not pulling my weight around here, and you're suffering for it." She had to be. If Ben slacked off, more responsibility fell on Melissa's shoulders. "That's not fair of me. I promise to change from now on. No more shirking duties for Ben Cowley. As of tomorrow I'm back on my game. Ready to take on the world and win."

"You don't need to do this alone, you know?"

"Course I do. I was the one who slacked off, I'll be the one to correct my mistakes."

"We're a team, Ben. We work together. If a problem arises, we solve it together. We have for the last two years. There's no reason we can't approach this situation in exactly the same way."

Typical Melissa. Always ready to lend a colleague a helping hand, to help others in need. But Ben's need wasn't work-related this time, so asking for her help didn't feel right. "Sure there is. Business is business. It involves both of us. This is personal. It's my issue. Not yours."

Melissa folded her arms under her breasts, letting her jacket hang down from her hand and trail past her waist to her legs. "When it affects your work, it's my issue too."

Her stance pulled Ben's attention away from her face once again. His gaze snagged on her breasts—which rested prettily above her arms—before trailing down to her legs. She had good legs. Slim calves and feminine ankles that looked fine in heels. The midleg length of her skirt revealed a shapely pair of knees.

Nice. Very nice.

She should show off her body more often. From what he'd seen of it tonight, it was a body worth showing off. Funny how he'd never noticed that before. But then he'd never taken the time to think of Melissa out of a work context before.

Why not?

She was smart, goal-oriented, a hard worker, always available to the staff who reported to her. He'd heard nothing but praise from their colleagues, and felt nothing but respect himself. In fact, she reminded him of himself. Not the well-respected part, but the goal-oriented, driven bit. She was so like him at work, the two of them would probably get along famously if they ever tried to be friends.

Why had they never tried to be friends? Apart from a little office flirting, Ben had never even considered the idea.

"So you have a solution to my hardness, anger and tension?"

Melissa nodded slowly, thoughtfully. "Actually, I do."

Ben couldn't resist flirting, couldn't resist the urge to bring a smile to her face. He wanted to see what she looked like with her luscious lips curved into a big grin and framed by that mane of beautiful hair. Or maybe he wanted to turn the focus of their conversation away from him. "So let's see. You think the first step to solving my problem lies in getting laid. I need to have sex." He nodded once. "And what? You're offering to be the one I have sex with?"

He grinned at her, waiting for those cheeks to turn the light pink he knew they would. The blush would only last a few seconds. Just until she realized he was teasing. And then maybe, just maybe, she'd be amused by his comment and smile for him.

The blush never came, but the smile did, and it smacked Ben right in the middle of his stomach. "That's exactly what I'm offering."

Ben hesitated for just a second before he realized she'd turned the tables on him, and she was the one doing the teasing. He smiled too. "Good one, Sparks. For a minute there I thought you were being serious."

Her smile faltered. "I am, Ben. I'm deadly serious."

Ben laughed out loud. "You know, you're right. I have been too uptight lately. I needed something to break the tension. Thank you for giving me something to laugh about."

Melissa ran a tongue over her upper lip so it glistened even more. She walked over to the chair on the other side of his desk and laid her jacket upon it. "You should know me better than that, Ben. I never joke when it comes to finding solutions to problems. You have a problem, and I have the solution. You need a woman, and it just so happens...I am one." To prove her point, she slipped open the first three buttons on her blouse, allowing Ben a healthy glimpse of what lay beneath—a tight, white camisole that covered the full curves of her breasts.

Ben's jaw dropped.

That was all it took for him to get an erection. With a sudden rush of blood, his cock filled and stiffened, leaving him perplexed.

A stiffy?

For Melissa?

Considering friendship was one thing. Being hit for six by an unexpected dose of lust another altogether.

"Now please don't mistake this for anything it's not," Melissa told him. "It's not as if I'm going to start bringing food into work for you." She rolled her eyes, mocking herself. "That's a good thing, by the way. I'm a terrible cook." Her smile was small, but it still lit up his office. "And I'm not going to get all soppy and lovey-dovey on you either." She spoke more seriously now. "This is just one solution. Sex. That's all, nothing more."

Ben gaped at her. Sex? Melissa Sparks was offering to have sex with him?

She smiled again. This time with a seductive, sexy expression he'd never dreamed he'd see on her face—not directed at him anyway. The smile was just as enchanting as the previous one. "You look surprised."

"Er, a little surprised, yeah." Even more surprising was the fact he could form words. Melissa? Seducing him?

Melissa undid the rest of her buttons and pushed the shirt off her shoulders, so she was now clad from the waist up in just the camisole.

Fuck, she looked sexy. Damn sexy. Sexy in a way Melissa had never looked to Ben. Uh—not just sexy. She was prime female flesh. All woman. And she did crazy things to his insides.

She made breathing difficult. Made him wonder if someone had messed with the air conditioning, because the temperature seemed to have jumped about twenty degrees in the last couple of minutes.

Ben was forced to loosen his tie and undo his top button. Anything to get fresh air on his feverish skin.

"Here's the deal—assuming you agree, because this would involve both of us." Melissa pulled the cami up and over her shoulders, leaving her breasts covered by nothing more than a satiny white bra.

Holy shit. She had a pair on her.

So not what he should be concentrating on. He should be remembering that she was a colleague. An excellent investment banker. A woman who'd given him outstanding advice and support over the years.

"You get to fuck me whenever the stress and tension get to be too much. This won't be a relationship. Well, not a traditional relationship, anyway. This'll just be a natural extension of our working association. We work, we fuck, we go home. End of story. I'm not interested in deep and meaningfuls."

Melissa ducked her head as she said that, but Ben still caught a glimpse of some unidentifiable emotion in her eyes. Sadness? Loneliness? Determination? He couldn't tell.

She released the clasp and zip on her skirt and stepped out of it gracefully. "I am, however, focused on making partner. Which means my romantic life's suffered because I work ridiculous hours. But, see, I'm just as human as you are." She blushed, telling him that as focused as she was on making her little speech, her actions still embarrassed her a little.

Shy? Melissa? Well, there was a fascinating new insight into her.

He liked that shyness. A lot. Liked her uncertainty. Melissa never seemed uncertain.

"I have needs," Melissa said, still with the delightful pink stain on her cheeks. "You have needs. Let's meet those needs together and not get involved any deeper than that. What do you say?"

Ben wanted to respond. Christ, he wanted to badly, but first off, he wasn't sure what he'd say, and secondly he couldn't find his voice. His mouth was suddenly parched.

Garters?

His straight-laced colleague wore thigh-highs and garters under those practical skirts? Garters that matched her bra and knickers and made her legs look a mile long, by the way.

How could he not have known that?

A bead of perspiration slid down his spine.

Don't go there, Cowley. Don't make Melissa into another faceless woman you can fuck and walk away from. She deserved more than that.

She arched an eyebrow. The direct look combined with the light flush of her cheeks was most becoming on his colleague. "You're very quiet."

"Uh, lost for words." Ben shook his head. "Either that, or I'm having my first hallucination."

Melissa tilted her head to the side, looking uncertain. "A bad hallucination?"

Oh, yeah. He liked this shy Melissa a lot. "Hell, no. More like a wet dream."

Shy Melissa vanished. "I can deal with wet dreams. But I'd prefer to make this real." She lost the bra.

Ben stared helplessly. She was not making it easy for him to keep his distance.

Fuck me.

In his life, he'd never seen breasts like that. Full. Round. Firm. With nipples that just begged to be sucked on. Sienna had beautiful breasts too, but her body was so very different from Melissa's. Sienna was all soft, lush curves. Melissa was tall and slender, lean and toned. Her body had been sculpted from hours of running every morning—Ben knew this because sometimes Melissa arrived at work in her jogging clothes. There was not a drop of fat anywhere to be seen.

He'd always loved Sienna's curves, loved how womanly they were. Melissa's body was way more athletic, less giving, but no less appealing. Fact of the matter was, Ben's mouth was watering. For the first time in a year, hell in more—eight or nine years—he didn't want soft, lush curves. He wanted long, lean, toned thighs wrapped around his waist, and he wanted full, firm breasts in his mouth. Melissa's thighs and breasts.

He hadn't had that reaction to a single other woman he'd slept with in Sydney.

"Jesus, Melissa." He rasped out her name. "You're not fucking around here, are you?" He half expected her to break into laughter and yell out, *"You've just been Punk'd."*

She stared drolly at him. "Have you ever known me to fuck around?"

"Good point." Even the shy Melissa had gotten straight down to business. Er, pleasure.

He swiped his hand through his hair. Hell, he wanted to put that hand on his cock, rub it, pump it, do anything to relieve the pressure that grew with every passing second. Maybe if he relieved the pressure, he wouldn't feel so compelled to take Melissa up on her offer. "You're dead serious about this, then?"

She regarded him in silence before skirting around his desk, nudging his chair back a little and squeezing in between him and the desk. Then she pushed his laptop out of the way and hoisted herself up, sitting right where the computer had been a second ago. "Does this answer your question?" She placed a foot on each arm of his chair.

Her long, toned legs were covered in sheer, silky thigh-highs, making her skin glow golden beneath them.

Ben began to sweat in earnest. Beads of perspiration lined his upper lip and forehead.

This wasn't right. He shouldn't objectify her like this, like he'd been doing with every other woman since Sienna.

But he couldn't remember the last time he'd wanted someone this badly. Mind you, yeah, he could. What he couldn't believe was wanting another woman as much as he wanted Sienna. And the fact that the other woman was Melissa Sparks...

That just blew his mind.

There was no denying the low-grade ache in his cock or the straining in his balls. And there was no denying the sweet scent of arousal that drifted through the air. After working with Melissa this long, he'd become familiar with the cinnamony-vanilla fragrance of her perfume. He'd always found it pleasant. But he'd never known her to smell quite so...tempting.

It did his head in. Made his mouth water.

Never mind her breasts, he wanted to pull her white, satin knickers aside and sweep his tongue over the folds of her pussy.

"Sparks...er, Melissa, you know if we make this...deal, we can't go back? We can never be just work colleagues again. If I fuck you now..." He had to let the sentence drift off, had to catch his breath, because the thought of fucking her had pretty much paralyzed his lungs. He wanted her so badly, his chest burned. "If we sleep together, everything will change."

She bit her lower lip as she looked at him, considering his words. "Sleeping together implies sharing a bed and getting some shuteye. Look, Ben, I'm not interested in a nap. Or a full night's rest, for that matter." The blush that had stained her cheeks now spread enticingly over her neck. "I want a quick, hard fuck. I want as much pleasure as you can give me over the next half an hour or so, and then I want to go home, alone. Believe me, nothing will change at work. I won't let it. I'll be just the same person I was this afternoon, and yesterday afternoon and every afternoon before that. The only difference will be at night. When everyone's gone home—like they have now. Then we can act differently." She trailed her fingers over her breast, making the nipple harden. "And then, Ben, feel free to act however you like."

"Damn it, woman," he growled. "You have no idea how I want to act." Flashes of the life he'd led since coming to Sydney assailed him. Pictures of the debauchery he'd indulged in.

"Tell me," she purred.

"You're treading on dangerous ground." Ben's cock ached like blazes. He was more aroused then he had been in a year. Add to that the fact his already eccentric tastes and desires had become even more kinky since his last encounter with Sienna, and Melissa had very little clue what ground she trod on.

"Far as I can see, I'm not treading ground at all. I'm sitting in front of you, in your office, with my feet on your chair."

"And your legs spread temptingly before me." He was losing control. Letting lust get the better of his sensible judgment.

"You think that's tempting?" She raised an eyebrow and smiled another quick little smile.

Christ, he loved her smiles.

He nodded once. Very tempting. Made even more so by the fact that they were at work, and there was a good possibility someone could walk in on them. More than once Ben had left an important document at the office, forcing him to return once he'd already arrived home. If he could do it, anyone could. "You're like a little package asking to be unwrapped."

"Unwrap me," she urged.

"Melissa—"

"Mel."

He dragged his gaze away from the tempting package to look into her eyes. "Mel?"

"You're about to fuck me. I think we can drop the formalities."

"Mel..." That might take a little getting used to. "You took a chance coming here like this." Hell, just the thought that she had taken such a risk turned him on more. "What if I'd said no?"

"If I'd thought for a moment you'd say no, I'd have gone no further than letting my hair down."

"You knew I wouldn't turn you away?"

She leaned forward. "You should know by now I never jump into any deal without doing a background check first. I watched you, observed your reactions. Carefully. The second I pulled the clips from my hair, your eyes turned a shade darker and your cheeks reddened." Her hand hovered in the air between them and then landed on his shirt. "Your breathing has been uneven ever since. And now?" She smiled that sexy smile again. "Now it's just plain ragged. And that, Cowley, is a huge turn-on."

Christ, that speech just made him hornier. She'd observed him, summed up the situation and only then acted. Exactly what he'd do. "Course my breathing is a little ragged. Every time I inhale, I smell your pussy."

"Touch it," she whispered.

"Touch what?"

"My pussy."

Ben set his jaw in a firm line and curled his fingers into two fists, making sure he did not respond to the invitation. Not yet anyway. "Melis...Mel, you need to be sure." No fucking way in hell was he taking the deal if the woman wasn't one hundred percent certain. She may believe everything would go back to normal in the morning, everything would just be work as usual, but Ben knew better. Sex changed everything. And his and Melissa's relationship would be changed.

Melissa didn't answer. She pushed off his shoulders and lay back on his desk, leaving herself exposed to Ben's gaze.

A bead of sweat trailed down his spine. "Jesus, fuck. Okay, Sparks. You've got it. You have a deal."

She wanted him to touch her? So help her God, he'd touch her. But on his terms. In his own way.

He pulled his chair in close, placed his hands beneath her arse—cupping two handfuls of silky skin and firm butt cheeks—and lifted her groin to his face. His lips met the sodden juncture of her knickers—er, G-string, based on the feel of all that silken skin in his palms right now—and a groan filled the air. His or hers, he wasn't sure.

Well, hell.

The smell.

The taste.

The texture.

The satin crotch of her knickers was soaked through with her juices, and the nectar was enough to make him part his lips and suck.

Mel moaned and ground her pussy against his mouth.

Shit. Not enough, not even close to enough.

He didn't want his fill of satin. He wanted his fill of Melissa Sparks. Hooking a finger beneath the crotch of her knickers, he pulled them aside, exposing her swollen, pink folds.

If he'd thought the scent had been tempting from afar, the aroma up close was intoxicating.

He buried his face in her pussy and gorged, licking away every trace of her juices. He laved her folds clean and then headed to the source, dipping his tongue in her entrance and feasting on her from the inside.

God, he couldn't remember a woman ever tasting this good. This tempting. Couldn't remember wanting to consume someone whole.

Was it because he already knew her? Already admired her? Was it because the whole experience was so unexpected, so surreal, it only increased his desire? Or did Melissa really taste this good?

Ben couldn't get enough of her. He just wanted more. Wanted to sample every part of her. But that would mean stripping off those garters, and God help him, he just couldn't bring himself to get rid of them. Not when they ratcheted up his arousal about a thousand percent or more.

He settled for sampling her clit, running his tongue over it and around it. Lightly at first, then a bit more firmly.

Then not at all.

He pulled back and watched her squirm. Watched her twist her hips and push her pussy up at him. Listened to her soft moans and breathless begging. Let her need and desperation build. Let her juices flow freely again, so that when he acquiesced and licked her once more, he got a whole new mouthful of her arousal.

He couldn't neglect her clit. Not now. Not when she writhed and beseeched him to lick it.

Hearing Melissa beg was a potent aphrodisiac.

He gave it all of his attention, laving it over and over, harder and harder, until her words became meaningless and her groans grew louder, and she broke beneath his ministrations, climaxing under his tongue.

As shudders claimed her body and she bucked on the table, Ben released one of her buttocks, freeing a hand in order to ease the pressure in his cock. He opened his pants, pushed his boxers down as far as they could go and grasped his half-freed shaft.

He shivered violently with the need to come. A few hard jerks with his palm and he could spill. That was all he needed.

But if he climaxed now, it would be game over. And he'd barely even started playing. No way was he ending things anytime soon. He'd just discovered a whole new side to Melissa, a side he found outrageously appealing. He wanted to become better acquainted with her.

He let endless seconds pass, waiting for Mel to come down to earth.

When she did, when her pussy stopped pulsing and her back relaxed against the desk, he simply resumed his feast, licking her all over again, dipping into her dripping channel, tasting her sweetness, teasing her clit. He teased her and laved her and fucked her with his tongue, loving how worked up she got.

All the while he pumped his shaft carefully, relieving his own tension without calling a premature end to the proceedings.

But as she panted before him, her pussy swollen and gleaming beneath his gaze, his hand could no longer give him what he needed. His blood pressure was rising fast. If he held back any longer, he'd likely have a stroke.

Chapter Two

Ben yanked the drawer of his desk open, frantically searching for his wallet. It took long, painful seconds to find it in this state, but finally he had it—and the condom he always kept there—in his greedy fingers.

He jumped to his feet, pushing off his pants and boxers, and sheathed himself in record time. He considered thrusting immediately, lodging himself deep inside her, but deferred it for a minute.

Once again he dipped his head down and licked Melissa's pussy until she shivered in excitement. Until the muscles in her thighs began to tense and her back arched, pushing her exquisite breasts upwards. Seconds before another orgasm could overwhelm her, he pulled away, leaving her unsatisfied and unfulfilled.

She let him have it, complaining viciously, demanding more, demanding satisfaction, swearing. The expressions that came from her were nothing less than filthy. And filth like that—from the mouth of a straight-laced woman like Melissa— turned Ben on so much a strangled groan burst from his throat.

"You sure you want me to fuck you with my mouth?" His throat was raw with need. "You want me to shove my fingers in your cunt and make you scream?" Her description, not his, but hearing it must have turned his balls four different shades of blue, for sure. Christ, he needed to come. Needed relief. Needed to sheathe himself in Melissa's slick pussy and fuck her until they both exploded.

Jess Dee

"See, I think what you want in that delicious cunt of yours is not my tongue or my fingers. I think you want my dick. And I think you want it buried so deep you see stars."

A loud moan rent the air. "God, yes, I want your cock."

"Sit up, Mel." His tone brooked no argument, and he placed his hands in hers, giving her something to pull herself up with. It was with a small measure of relief he found himself in control of the situation. He'd been so blown away by her proposal, he'd let her lead him right where she wanted him to go.

Not that he was complaining. This was where he wanted to be too.

But Ben liked to be in control. Liked to ensure he had a firm hand on every situation. Liked to know he acted only after assessing every single detail. He hadn't assessed very much now. He'd been so overwhelmed by discovering these other sides to Melissa, he'd allowed her to take control.

The minute she sat upright, he had his hands on her breasts, molding his palms to the firm mounds, filling his grasp with them. Hell, they felt even better than they looked. They made him want to push them together, bury his cock between them and thrust until he came all over her neck. Made him want to suckle her nipples until she came from nothing more than the stimulation of her tits.

Ben strongly suspected that in this state, *he* could come just from sucking on her nipples. He was close. Too damn close. He needed to leave her breasts alone.

Ben dropped his hands to her thighs, relishing the softness of her thigh-highs and the sharper clasps of the garters. "Shift your arse closer to the edge of the desk and wrap your legs around my waist."

Huh, him giving Melissa instructions? It felt odd. And exciting.

28

She responded, folding her arms around his neck at the same time, pressing herself against him, chest to chest.

The instant she moved, his cock encountered her slick heat. The condom provided only the slightest barrier against all that liquid fire, and her touch burned straight through him. Her breasts pushed against his shirt and chest.

How could one woman feel so good? So right in his arms?

How could a colleague make him hotter, more aroused, then he'd ever been?

How could he not have suspected Melissa had all these devilishly attractive sides to her?

How could Ben think at a time like this? Was he crazy?

He broadened his stance, spreading his legs wider, so the head of his cock was exactly level with her slit, and tried to slow his wild panting.

"Know what the irony is?" Melissa whispered, her warm breath searing the very skin on his face. "With your mouth this close, now every time *I* inhale, I smell my pussy."

Ben groaned. He had no idea who moved first. Probably him, but maybe her. What he did know was that his lips were crushed against hers, and she'd opened her mouth to meet his fierce kiss.

Her tongue tasted as good as her pussy. As fresh as a breath of midnight air after a summer rainstorm. He danced his tongue over hers, feeding her back her own precious drops of honey, and she accepted them hungrily.

The kiss might be sweet, but it was also dirty. Just like her words a few minutes back. As she feasted on his mouth, she rubbed her pussy against his throbbing cock, engulfing his tip with her lips and then freeing him, only to start all over again. Repeating the motion once, twice, twenty times, until blood roared in Ben's ears. He was lost to the incredible sensations. Lost to the hunger, the tease. The need. The ache.

The next time she caught his cockhead between her pussy lips, he couldn't hold back. He thrust once, hard, seating himself deep inside her body.

So good.

Fucking amazing.

Tight. Wet. Slippery.

Perfect. So fucking perfect.

Her inner muscles squeezed his cock, held it inside, tortured him. He growled into her mouth, pulled out and thrust back inside her.

Melissa dug her nails into his neck. Her legs tightened around his waist, drawing him closer, deeper inside. She broke the kiss, flung her head back and cried out in pleasure. A shock of russet hair cascaded behind her.

Fresh blood surged to his cock. How could he ever have perceived this sex goddess as straight-laced? How could he ever have seen her as anything other than the exquisite, provocative siren she was?

How could he never have considered doing this with her before? Now that Ben had had a taste of his tempestuous, enthralling colleague, he never wanted to let her go.

"Fuck me, Ben. Don't stop."

Stop? Not in a million years. He snapped his hips in controlled, deliberate actions, aimed at filling her at just the right angle, caressing her G-spot, providing maximum pleasure. He lost himself to the rhythm of their movements and to her slick, enticing heat.

What began as an attempt to drive her into a delirious frenzy of desire backfired. It wasn't Melissa who was being driven crazy, it was him.

He was losing his mind to the pleasure, losing his concentration. Spinning out of control—again. He couldn't think inside her, couldn't focus. She felt too damn amazing wrapped around him like that, the walls of her pussy constricting against his cock, her legs crushing his waist, her arms holding him so damned tight.

He was surrounded by one-hundred-percent, absolute female. And at that point he wasn't sure which side of her turned him on more. The siren, the brilliant investment banker, or the shy woman?

His orgasm built. His cock ached, his balls grew taut. Hell, he was going to come, he couldn't stave it off. Didn't have the willpower. He couldn't hold back with all of this perfection wrapped around him.

"Mel—"

"Feels so good, Ben. S-so good." Her shallow pants filled the air. "Faster," she demanded, "harder."

Huh. As if he had any choice. As if he'd intended to move any other way. He slammed into her, going so deep his balls slapped her arse, going so fast he forgot to breathe, didn't have time.

Pleasure clouded his vision. He couldn't see, couldn't think. All he could do was feel, and that feeling was the closest thing to euphoria he'd ever experienced.

He was on the edge, losing it. He couldn't hold off.

"Melissa!" He groaned her name, then ground his teeth together hard, trying not to lose it.

Not before her. He couldn't, wouldn't. It wasn't fair to take his pleasure first.

Oh, Christ. It might not be fair but neither was it

preventable. He couldn't stop it. Couldn't hold back.

The orgasm slammed through him, hauling the breath from his body. He could no more have prevented it than he could have pulled away from her. He came hard. So hard he couldn't keep his eyes open. Couldn't breathe, couldn't think.

Couldn't...

Oh, God. Oh, fuck. So good. So fucking good.

Made even more extraordinary by the fact that as he climaxed, in dizzying blasts of pleasure, Melissa came too.

Her pussy clasped his pumping cock like a tight fist. Clenching rhythmically around him, coaxing every last drop of come he had to give.

As the pleasure tore through him, accessing every nerve in his body, Melissa screamed, surrendering to her orgasm.

Seconds before his knees gave in beneath him, he hauled Melissa off the desk and collapsed back into his chair—with his colleague still wrapped around his dick.

He groaned at the sweet agony of it all. His cock, now spent inside her, was too sensitive to stand even the slightest jarring. Melissa's erratic shivers made the experience nothing less than excruciating. Beautifully, electrifyingly excruciating.

Gasping, searching for breath and inhaling only the heady scent of musk and sex, Ben realized one thing. He had just had the most powerful orgasm of his life—with his colleague.

For long moments they sat together, panting, regaining their equilibrium. His body might be too exhausted to move, but his mind was flying. A million thoughts ran through his head. Melissa was mad if she thought for one second their relationship could ever go back to what it had been just minutes ago.

He'd always stood in awe of her professional ability, her

work ethic, her leadership skills, her straightforward attitude and her business acumen. Now that he'd seen other facets of her personality and had a taste of her, he somehow doubted he could let her go. And just as soon as he had the energy to speak, he'd tell her as much.

Only his energy did not return fast enough. While he still fought for breath, Melissa gracefully disentangled herself from his arms.

He tried to hold on to her, tried to clasp her close, but she pulled away, climbing off his lap, and the distraction of losing all that heat around his cock proved too much.

He let Melissa escape.

She stood up, straightened her knickers and smoothed down her hair. Then she leaned over and gave Ben one final kiss. A flick of her tongue over his, a swift melding of their lips, and it was over.

A kiss far too chaste and far too quick to ever satisfy him after what they'd just shared.

"I hope that was a step in the right direction." She smiled. "Maybe now you can start to feel a little happier again?" She walked around the desk, collecting the clothes she'd discarded earlier. "It sure helped me. I feel...freer. You more than met my needs. I hope I met yours?" The look she shot him was inquiring, as though she'd just asked about one of their business deals.

Ben gaped at her, uncertain how to respond. She looked...awkward, as though she wasn't sure what to say or do now, how to behave. So she'd reverted straight back to the professional—just like he'd have done under similar circumstances.

She shrugged off his silence, dressing quickly and efficiently, doing up every last button and replacing her jacket.

"W-we can do this again if you'd like. Perhaps next week?"

Her cheeks were rosy from their passion, but as she spoke, they reddened further.

Ah. There she was. Shy Melissa. Endearing Melissa. He thought he'd lost her.

Ben shook his head fiercely.

Disappointment flashed through her eyes but disappeared as soon as she blinked. "You don't want to do it again?"

"Don't want to wait until next week," he said with a soft growl. Christ, he didn't want to wait another five minutes. He wanted to rip her clothes off and fuck her all over again, right now.

But the second she'd climbed off his lap, she'd changed. She'd slipped right back into her business persona. She was formal, a little distant and a different woman from the filthy sex kitten who'd insisted he shove his tongue in her cunt.

In fact, the only thing different about her now from when she'd first walked into his office was the riotous mass of hair around her shoulders. And the heightened color in her cheeks. Even her jacket was buttoned up, hiding any hint of the extraordinary breasts he ached to touch again.

"Well, maybe tomorrow night, then?" she asked. "I'll just check my calendar and make sure I have nothing else scheduled. If not, shall we say ten p.m., your office?"

He blinked. "Back to formalities so quickly?"

"The sex is over for now. It's business as usual." She softened her voice. "I told you, Ben, nothing would change about our working relationship."

Ben glanced down at his naked groin, his limp dick still covered in the used condom. He grabbed a couple of tissues, rolled it off then scrunched it in his fist. "There's nothing usual about this, goddammit."

She wrinkled her nose and for the briefest moment looked surprised. "No there isn't, is there?" Then she straightened her shoulders. "Never mind, it'll become routine. Like anything else, the more we do it, the more normal it will feel. Right?" Without waiting for his answer, she launched into her next question. "Now, about tomorrow night? Yes? No?"

He glared at her, unwilling to answer. No way was she taking what they'd just shared—the most incredible sex—and trivializing it into a business proposition.

She frowned. "Should I take your silence as a no?"

Ben snarled. This was not how he'd envisioned things when she first stripped off her shirt. He had no idea what he'd envisioned. But losing the sensual, shy siren to this aloof, awkward work mate wasn't what he wanted.

She sighed, and in that sigh he heard a hint of the sex kitten. "That's a pity. I'd kind of started anticipating it already. Never mind. If it doesn't suit you, it doesn't suit you. I can always use my vibrator instead. Perhaps in the bath." Was that a glint in her eyes? "Definitely in the bath. Anyway, goodnight, Ben. I'll see you in the morning. Sleep well." She ran her hand languidly through her long hair and smiled. "I know I will."

And with that she turned and walked to the door.

"Melissa," Ben barked at her, way louder than he'd meant to. Hell, he was out of control. Off balance. His world was out of whack.

She paused and turned to face him, one foot in the office, one out.

"Yes," he growled.

She shook her head in confusion. "Yes, what?"

"Yes to tomorrow night." Because what else could he say

when his dick was already rising again from the image she'd planted in his head of herself in the bath? "Ten p.m., in my office."

"Oh. Okay then." She nodded once. And smiled. A smile that not only lit up the interior of his office, it warmed him all over. "Night," she said, and walked away.

Just before she disappeared around a corner, Ben found the energy to yell one command at her. "And bring your goddamned vibrator with you!"

The slight hesitation in her step was the only indication she gave him that she'd heard. Then Melissa disappeared from his line of vision.

Ten minutes later Melissa stumbled through the public car park, fumbled with her keys and collapsed into the front seat of her car, her heart smashing against her ribs.

Dear God, she'd done it. Given in to her persistent craving for Ben Cowley and seduced him. She hadn't meant to. Had never intended to expose even the slightest bit of her feelings about him.

For over two years she'd kept her emotions hidden. Refused to allow anyone to know she had a ridiculous crush on Ben. It had developed the first day she'd met him, the first time he'd introduced himself.

Even then—when he'd been so in love with his girlfriend—she'd felt the pull. And the envy. When Ben had spoken about Sienna, his face had shone. Love seemed to radiate from him. How incredible it must have been for Sienna to feel loved like that. To wake up every morning in her man's arms, knowing she was the focus of his world.

Melissa hadn't known love like that for a very long time. Hadn't let anyone get close enough. Even after Sienna and Ben broke up, Melissa had kept her distance. It was one thing perving over a colleague from afar. It was another letting her emotions interfere with a successful business relationship.

Besides, Ben was out of her league. He was a man who thrived on social interaction. Who was at his happiest with the woman he loved. Melissa was the opposite. She was most successful when she operated alone. When she let no one close, allowed herself no distractions.

There'd been a time when she'd allowed herself every distraction under the sun. And it had nearly ruined her.

Not nearly. It had broken her. Destroyed everything she'd once been, and left her life shattered. Picking up the pieces had been a long, hard and lonely job.

The loneliness got to her. It gnawed away at her slowly and constantly. And this evening, that loneliness, combined with an argument with her mother, had succeeded in working her up into a fine tizz. She'd needed to blow off steam. Needed to step out of her life for a minute. Needed to be anyone but Melissa Sparks.

And what better way to escape from her life than to act in the least predictable way imaginable? No one would *ever* expect her to seduce Ben—least of all her—so that was what she'd done. She'd gone against the grain. For the first time in forever she'd given in to her deepest, most hidden needs and done what she'd wanted. Distracted herself. In one big way.

Her hands shook like crazy. They shook so much she couldn't even start the car. If she tried to drive in this condition, she'd have an accident.

The day Ben had transferred to head office and informed her about his split with Sienna, Melissa's feelings for him had

Jess Dee

run rampant. Never mind hiding her puppy eyes from him, she'd barely been able to control the desire and the longing that seeped through every cell of her body.

Tonight she'd snapped. She'd taken one look at him sitting alone in his office and accepted that she couldn't exist another minute without knowing what it would be like to touch Ben. Kiss him. Fuck him. Be fucked by him.

Long before stepping into his office she'd accepted that she'd never know what it would feel like to be loved by him, but she had an opportunity to discover what making love to him would be like.

And now she knew.

She drew in a shuddery breath. The sex had been worth the two-year wait. And the knowledge that she could do it all over again tomorrow night...

A wild tremor shuddered through her. Her pussy throbbed and her nipples tingled, excitement at the prospect making her dizzy.

A fresh wave of arousal washed over her.

Okay, so maybe it wasn't just arousal. Maybe it was her way of expressing all those feelings she'd held inside for so long. She couldn't show them emotionally, so they came out physically.

They were potent. Too potent to ignore. And her pussy—still tingling from Ben's mouth and cock—once again ached to be stroked. Hidden in her car, in the almost empty parking lot, she couldn't resist the temptation.

She dropped her head back against the seat, closed her eyes and let her hand creep beneath her skirt. She shifted once so she could reach, pushed her G-string out of the way, and her finger was on her clit, caressing, rubbing, teasing.

It didn't take long. She was too worked up. Too emotionally charged. A minute, maybe less. A minute filled with memories of the long, wet strokes of Ben's tongue and the deep, hard thrusts of his cock. Of Ben, the guy she'd dreamed about for years. Memories of his arousal, of the lust that had darkened his eyes and made him sweat.

Of the sound of his groans and her cries as he'd filled her, fucked her. The feel of his release rocking his entire body, his cock pulsing in her cunt, over and over. The mindless calling of her name.

The sound of it, echoing through his office, had been the final push. She'd plunged over the edge and fallen into the deep abyss of ecstasy.

Sitting in the car, with the memories washing through her, Melissa came again.

She came fast, and she came hard, and it took a good few seconds before she could open her eyes, before she could take a few steadying gulps of air. Before her arms were steady enough to put the key in the ignition and start the car. Before she trusted herself to drive without smashing into anything or anyone.

When she finally threw the gear into reverse and looked around to make sure her path was clear, shock slammed through her. About ten bays down, a man—a stranger—leaned against his car watching her.

Melissa's heart skipped a beat.

He'd seen her expression as she'd masturbated. Recognized what she'd done. For sure. The knowing smile on his face told her as much.

Melissa hit the accelerator, peeling out of the car park. As she drove, pressing her foot down too hard and too recklessly, she knew she should feel ashamed. And embarrassed. She knew she should regret what she'd just done.

But she didn't. Couldn't.

She'd relieved so much tension, so much inner turmoil, she couldn't regret it. Besides, the knowledge that someone had watched her reliving her glorious moments with Ben only heightened the extreme pleasure of the entire evening. As dirty and as smutty as it was, Melissa hadn't felt so free in a very long time. She loved the fact that she and Ben had fucked, and she loved the fact that someone had watched her touch herself.

For the first time since she was eighteen, Melissa felt satisfied. Felt as though she'd finally done something she'd wanted to do—and been rewarded for it very richly indeed.

Chapter Three

Slow down.

Take a deep breath.

Act normal.

Melissa looked sedately over her desk as Ben shut the door tight and made sure it stayed closed.

Oh, God. How could she act normally when her heart thundered like crazy? When just seeing him made her smile, made her feel as carefree as she had last night?

"Cowley," she said by way of greeting.

"We need to talk." Ben stalked across the room, leaned over her desk and rested his fingertips on it. He seemed agitated and out of sorts.

Alarm bells went off in her head. Ben was in her office, which must mean he needed to discuss work. Much as she'd have loved for him to visit her in her office just to chat, it had never happened. She'd never thought to allow it. "Did something happen with the Everton bond?"

Everton & Everton had been sitting on the fence for the last two weeks, weighing up their options about going ahead and issuing debt. Ben had given them a deadline for a decision, and from the expression on his face now, she suspected the decision they'd made wasn't the one she and Ben had hoped for.

"This has nothing to do with Everton." He shook his head impatiently. "This has to do with us. Last night."

Outwardly, Melissa checked her watch. It was eleven in the

morning, which meant it was slap bang in the middle of a workday. This was neither the time nor the place to make small talk about last night. No matter how agitated Ben might be. She'd told him she would keep their relationship professional, promised nothing would change. She had to stick to her word.

Inwardly, her stomach twisted into an excited knot. This may not be the time or place to talk about it, but the very thought that Ben wanted to discuss last night made her dizzy with anticipation. Ben wanted to talk to her about something unrelated to work. Hurrah.

It so couldn't happen.

She couldn't let him cross the boundaries she'd been so careful to draw. Because if she did, she'd let her guard down. She'd let him in. She'd grow distracted. And she couldn't afford to be distracted from her goals again.

Mel threw up a desperate hand. "No, Ben, please. Don't bring this up now. By all means, we can discuss what happened, but we need to do it later. Outside of business hours, when the offices are deserted."

If she redrew the line in the sand then Ben couldn't step over it, right?

And neither could she, no matter how much she might want to.

A muscle ticked in his cheek. "This isn't something that can wait until then."

Her heart leapt, but she forced herself to both breathe and think calm thoughts. "Is it a matter of life or death?" Her greedy gaze devoured every inch of his gorgeous face, from his short, jet-black hair to his chocolaty eyes, high cheekbones and oh-so-delicious lips.

"What? No."

"So no one will die if we don't discuss it now? Or suffer serious injury, at any rate?"

He grimaced. "No one's health will be risked or compromised in any way. But something happened that you need to know about."

"Did you change your mind?" Please, God, don't let him have changed his mind. She'd only just reached out to him. She didn't think she could bear it if he pushed her away so soon. "If you don't want to meet again tonight, that's perfectly fine," she lied.

Ben clenched his jaw, the muscles in his throat standing out in stark relief. "No, damn it, I didn't change my mind. But I received something that may change yours."

Her curiosity was piqued. She was desperate to know what he'd gotten. But if she gave in, if she let him speak about what they'd done, she'd never want him to stop. She suspected her walls would come crumbling down, and she'd focus on nothing else for the rest of the day.

She might even begin removing her jacket and shirt...

No. Better not to discuss anything now. No matter how pressing the matter. Befriending a colleague would distract her from her goals, and she had to stick to those no matter what. She had to make partner. Had to prove to the world, to herself, that she could do it. Prove to herself and everyone she knew she was no longer the failure she'd been in high school.

Besides, befriending Ben would inevitably lead to sex, because now that she'd had a taste of him, there was no way she could keep her hands off him. And fucking a colleague in her office, with everyone around, would in all probability lead to instant dismissal.

"Ben, whatever happens between us after office hours has to remain between us *after* office hours. During the day nothing

43

can change." A hint of desperation crept into her tone, and she chased it away. "Which means we don't get to talk about *us* while there's an office full of people or while there are contracts that need follow-up and businesses that need financing."

"Seriously?" Ben's eyes glittered. "You're not willing to acknowledge anything that happened? No matter how it might impact you? *Us?*"

Lord, she wanted to, so much. "Not now." Her voice was hoarser than she would have liked.

"You're not even the least bit curious to know what's so important?"

"God, of course I am." She was all but bursting. "But I can't allow myself to think about it now." Melissa had to get him out of her office before she caved in and begged him to tell her. Fortunately she had a perfect excuse—a meeting with their team's financial analyst. "I'm sorry, Ben, you need to leave. Alistair will be here any minute."

What she wanted, what she really wanted, was to invite Ben to sit down. To take a load off his feet, forget about the real world that waited for them outside her office door, and just keep her company.

She wanted to talk to him. Not just to hear what he needed to tell her, but to talk. Really talk. About anything and everything. To connect with him on a level that had nothing to do with work and nothing to do with sex. Okay, maybe a little to do with sex. Or even a lot. But at least the talk would be personal and intimate. It would be about them. Not about some business deal that she didn't give a damn about.

Melissa suppressed a sad sigh. It wasn't going to happen. She raised an eyebrow, awaiting his response.

Ben straightened, watching her in meditative silence. Then he shook his head and gave a short, empty laugh. "Fine, we'll play it your way. For now. No more talk about us. I'll see you in my office at ten tonight." He walked to the door. "But…if we're going to play it your way, then we're going to play it properly. So this time, when you walk into my office, come prepared."

"Prepared?"

He nodded. "No knickers. No bra. No shirt and no camisole. Leave the garters on. Wear any of the rest and the deal's off. Got it?"

Melissa nodded calmly, feeling anything but. "Got it." Arousal mixed with relief that Ben might want her again.

"Good. Now, one more thing." He stared straight into her eyes and wouldn't let her turn away. Not that she wanted to. In that instant, she could have spent the rest of her life looking into those eyes, seeing the steely resolve in them, the control, the flicker of lust he tried to blink away but couldn't. And the frustration. With her? "You better make damned sure the batteries of your vibrator are charged. You're going to need them."

A million hours passed before ten o'clock arrived. A million hours drenched in anticipation, concern and apprehension. Every time he looked at his desk, which was only *all* the time, Ben got an erection. Impossible not to as he recalled the mind-blowing activities he and Melissa had indulged in less than twenty-four hours ago.

At about eight, Ben began to feel antsy. What? Had everyone at Preston Elks decided to work late tonight? Was tomorrow deadline hell? Couldn't they just go home?

His thoughts disturbed him. Never before had the presence of someone else been a concern. When it came to sex in public, the risk of being caught was half the fun. But this was a work situation, and both he and Melissa were professionals. If they were caught while having the kind of sex Ben hoped to have with Melissa tonight, it would not only soil his reputation, it would wound hers as well.

And Ben was not prepared to put Melissa's outstanding reputation at risk.

As for the email he'd received that morning, well, hell. He'd read and reread it several times, unsure how to respond. In the end he hadn't answered at all. He couldn't, at least not until he'd spoken to Melissa and formulated an appropriate reply.

By nine thirty Ben was all but climbing the walls. Light still flared from intermittent offices down the corridor. By his count at least three people other than himself and Melissa were around.

There was just another half an hour. Would they be gone in time?

And if they weren't?

Shit, he didn't want to think about it. His balls couldn't stand the torture. Neither could his stomach. Much as Ben looked forward to fucking Melissa, he couldn't wait to see her again. Couldn't wait to see those other sides of her personality he found so attractive. Hell yeah, he wanted to bury himself inside of her, balls-deep, but he also wanted to find out more about her, get to know her a little better.

Perhaps develop a third relationship with her. Perhaps he and she could stand a chance of being friends as well as colleagues and sex buddies.

Funny, he hadn't wanted to get to know a single other woman he'd slept with since Sienna. What was it about Melissa that made him think differently?

He swiveled in his chair, staring out the window. At least it was dark outside. Oftentimes at night he'd see lights shining in the office that faced his, the office in the adjacent building. Tonight it was filled with nothing but shadows, a fact Ben found oddly consoling.

Or did he?

When the wait became unbearable, he made a trip to the men's room. Anything to pass the damn minutes. He couldn't recall the last time he'd looked so forward to seeing a woman. When he'd arrogantly gone after Sienna and tried to win back her love, there'd been an enormous sense of anticipation. But it had been tinged with doubt. She'd left him, and he'd had no guarantees she'd want to see him again.

Turned out she hadn't. Not really.

Melissa wanted to see him again. She was a sure thing. Okay, so a sure thing on her terms, not his, but those terms suited him just fine. No-strings-attached sex? Perfect. Just what he needed now. A harmless fling to help him get over Sienna once and for all. A fling with someone as different from Sienna as a woman could be, although each was outrageously sexy in her own right.

Hell, how much of a surprise had that been? Discovering that beneath all those prim suits of Melissa's was a firecracker just waiting to be lit. How much of a turn-on?

A huge fucking turn-on. A turn-on that had turned him into a livewire pretty much the entire day. He couldn't wait to get her naked again. Couldn't wait to sheathe his cock in her tight, wet pussy.

He took a slow walk back to his desk from the bathroom, and his relief at finding only one other person in the office was immeasurable. Mike Peters, a newly qualified accountant working under Ben, looked up as Ben tapped at his door.

"Putting in a few extra hours?"

Mike nodded. "Thought I'd get this report finished before

47

going home."

How many times had Ben thought something similar? "Work is important, Mike, but not more important than your friends and family. Don't neglect them for something that can wait until tomorrow."

"But if I do this now—"

"Take off, kid. You have your sister's wedding this weekend, right? Go spend some time with her. Go enjoy your family." If only he'd been given that advice once upon a time.

The young man nodded, closed his Excel spreadsheet and was out the door minutes later.

Which left the offices of Preston Elks all but deserted.

Ben was back in his chair maybe five minutes before Melissa made her entrance.

She didn't say a word. She simply stood in his doorway like she had last night, looking imposing and dressed to kill.

And hell, she about gave him a heart attack right then and there. She wore a charcoal, pinstriped skirt suit, with the jacket buttoned up in front, just like she had last night.

Last night, however, she'd hidden every asset with a severe white blouse and her jacket. Tonight, she had on absolutely nothing beneath her blazer. Which meant when she stood at that angle and folded her arms, the jacket gaped a little, giving him an enticing view of a full, firm breast and a dusky pink nipple.

Ben swallowed. Any greeting he might have spoken died in his throat. The wild mane of untamed hair was back. This time she'd lost her ponytail before leaving her office. Her lips were painted a deep, sexy red. His first once-over failed to reveal what the second one did: a pair of lacy knickers hanging off one of her fingers, and a white and blue object tucked comfortably into her other hand.

Just like that he was hard. Again.

"Melissa."

"Ben."

"I'm pleased to see you came prepared."

She arched an eyebrow. "Give me five minutes and you'll find a whole new reason to be pleased." Her smoky voice filled the room with promise.

"If you think five minutes is all we need, you're going to be sorely disappointed."

She cocked an eyebrow. "Somehow I doubt disappointment will feature as a key element in tonight's proceedings." A soft, electric buzz hummed through the air.

Ben's dick ached. The eternal wait for this moment, combined with the subtle fragrance of her perfume—cinnamon and vanilla—was proving too much for him. He wanted a piece of Melissa Sparks.

Nope, scratch that. He wanted all of Melissa Sparks, but now, with her dressed so enticingly, with the sensual promise of things to come in her voice, he wasn't exactly focused on everything.

He was focused on sex.

Snap out of it. Show some respect. Hell, show some dignity.

"You haven't asked me what I needed to tell you earlier."

She nodded. "I figured if it was that important you'd tell me in your own good time."

Cool as a cucumber. How did she do that? Act as though nothing in the world bothered her while he was burning up at about a million freaking degrees. Tonight she showed no hint of the woman who'd blushed more than once last night. "I received an email this morning."

"And?"

The buzz continued. Soft. Barely audible. "You need to read it." He turned his laptop so the screen faced her.

"Why don't you read it for me?" Melissa shifted her hand so the tip of the blue and white object she held slipped beneath the lapel of her jacket. *Her vibrator.* A sleek, chic, stylish vibrator intended purely for a woman's pleasure. "I'm...a little busy here."

Ben swallowed again, only this time his throat was dry as a bone, which only increased his discomfort.

Jesus, fuck.

The lapels of her jacket quivered. Color rose in her cheeks, and her pupils dilated.

Ben stifled a groan and pressed a hand to his balls, desperately trying to ease the strain there.

What the hell had happened to his straight-laced colleague? Could she have a twin sister he'd never known about? An identical twin who only came out to play at night? And so much for his plans to take control of the reins tonight. Yeah, she'd "obeyed" him and brought along the vibe. But instead of him using it to torment her, she was the one doing the tormenting.

He should have known she'd up the ante. She'd never have just heeded his instruction. Melissa would have looked at every possible way she and he could utilize the vibrator, and settled on choosing the one that would get the best response—from both of them.

She gave him an enquiring look. "The email?"

Ah, right. The email. He'd forgotten all about it. "You sure you don't want to see it for yourself?" It might be less embarrassing for her if she read it.

"Quite sure." She edged the vibe over to her other breast.

Okay, well, he'd given her the choice. He turned the computer back around. "It's short. A couple of lines. That's all." Christ, he'd about give his left testicle to see her slip her hand inside her skirt.

"I'm listening."

Was she? Her eyes had closed, and her color had heightened even further.

"It's from a, uh, friend of mine."

"Mm hm?"

"He works close by. In the building next door."

Ever so sensually, she tucked her knickers in her pocket and popped the buttons of her jacket, treating Ben to the unhindered sight of those exquisite breasts being tormented by the vibrator. Her nipples stood taut and hard, two perfect peaks begging to be kissed.

Ben sucked in a breath and thanked God for the darkness outside. Although a part of him, a very small part, almost wished light would glimmer through the two windows behind him. "His office overlooks mine."

"That's nice," Melissa said, definitely distracted. She lowered the hand with the toy in it so it trailed down over her belly, vibrating over her skin. Goosebumps covered every visible inch of her flesh.

And his. The non-visible bits too.

For long seconds he couldn't talk. All he could do was watch as she did what he'd desperately wanted her to do. She slipped the toy beneath the waistband of her skirt. Her arm moved slowly and then stopped.

Melissa moaned.

He had no doubt whatsoever the vibrator now rested

against her clit. Ben forgot to breathe.

Her skirt quivered.

"So, you going to read it or not?"

At least she had the presence of mind to ask. He had not an intelligible thought in his head. He cleared his throat and forced himself to concentrate on the screen.

"*Benny Boy...*"

Melissa's mouth twitched in the makings of a smile. "Benny Boy?"

"A nickname." He frowned. "Not the point of the email." But he appreciated the half smile anyway.

"Okay, go— *Oh...God!*" She arched her back, pushing her chest out in the process, displaying those exquisite breasts in all their aroused glory, telling Ben the vibe had touched a sensitive spot. "G-go on."

Goddamned lucky vibrator.

"*Benny Boy,*" he read, his voice so hoarse he had trouble articulating the words. "*That was quite some show you put on last night. Thoroughly enjoyed it. Same time tonight?*"

Melissa froze. She opened both eyes, staring at him in silence.

So quiet was she, the subdued sounds of the vibrator seemed to hum through the office.

"He saw us together." Ben eyed her carefully, looking for any hint of a reaction. "Watched everything we did to each other."

Her gaze skittered away from him to the window behind his chair, but other than that she did not respond.

Surprising. Maybe she hadn't registered his words. He went for a more blunt approach. "He saw me go down on you. Watched me lick your pussy."

Her gaze did not move from the window, and her lack of reaction worried him. He'd expected horror. Shame. Embarrassment. He got nothing of that.

"He stood there, looking through his window, the one directly opposite mine, when I stuck my tongue in your cunt."

She trembled, but still said not a word. Although she did whimper, and the sound sent shivers over his skin.

"He was there, with us, when I fucked you. He watched you come apart. Watched me climax inside you. He saw it all. Every last thing. He saw every dirty act we indulged in."

A soft gasp escaped her. She closed her eyes as she jerked, as though a sharp jolt had just gone through her body.

Shock?

Her head fell back and several more jolts shuddered through her. A keening sound filled the air. She grabbed the doorpost with her free hand.

Oh, fuck. Oh, Jesus.

Not shock. Not even close to shock.

Melissa was coming. Orgasming before his eyes. A real pleasurable orgasm, if the expression of rapture and the flush on her breasts and her neck were anything to go by. An orgasm brought about by the combination of his disclosure and her vibrator.

The woman had gotten off on hearing that someone had seen them last night.

Not just someone. Will.

Chapter Four

Ben swallowed hard, watching as tremors raced over her body, giving her time to come down from the high. He counted to ten, forcing back the desire that pitched tumultuously in his own groin.

When his breathing was under full control and he believed he could talk in a voice that would not resemble the growl of a bear, he spoke to her. "It's interesting. You never struck me as the type to get off on being watched." Delivered in a cool and calm demeanor. The exact opposite of how he felt.

"Apparently I never struck you as the type to seduce a colleague at work either." Melissa opened her eyes, looked at him with a gaze a good shade darker than usual and smiled. Her nipples stuck out proudly, evidence of the orgasm that had just ripped through her. Silence filtered through the room, telling him she'd switched off the vibe. "You have a lot to learn about me."

That he did. He wanted to learn everything about her. "Apparently. You willing to share anything else?" He'd take any scraps at this point. Anything she was willing to throw out to him.

"All in good time." Her gaze flickered away from his, back to the window. "Is...is he there now?"

Ah, Will. She was finally asking about him. He didn't turn around. "Is there light coming from his office?"

She shook her head. "It's dark."

"Then he's not there."

"Pity."

Ben took a sharp breath. Pity? "What if he was there?"

Melissa slipped her hand from her skirt, still holding the vibe. She stepped forward, heading straight to the window, where she trailed her fingers down it, from the top to the bottom. "I'd wave. Say hello."

"And then?" Close the blinds?

She did not avert her gaze, keeping it pinned on the darkness outside. "And then I'd lean into the window, like this." She twisted, resting the vibe on the window sill, right between her hands.

From this angle, Ben could see nothing but her jacket gaping open. Melissa's breasts were invisible to him, but if Will were sitting in his office, he'd be treated to a delectable view. Thank fuck he wasn't. Ben was in no mood to share. And thank fuck his window was hidden from the rest of the building. Will watching Melissa was one thing. But if anyone else had a view of her, he suspected he might want to kill them.

"And I'd shove my arse back like this." She shuffled her lower body back a step or two, so her spine arched and her slender rump stuck out appealingly. "Then I'd ask how you got to know the man in the office opposite you well enough for him to call you Benny Boy."

Ah, so now she wanted to talk? Fine by him. The more they spoke, the better he could get to know her. Ben licked his lips, his mouth dry from desire. "Ya know, if you tugged your skirt up above your hips, I might be tempted to tell you the answer."

Melissa studied him in silence. And then she wriggled her hips, tugging on her skirt with her left hand. Inch by torturous inch she exposed first her silken thigh, then her garters and finally her naked arse.

It took a good few seconds before Ben's heartbeat slowed

enough for him to stop shaking viciously.

Before pushing out of his seat, Ben removed a condom from his drawer and pocketed it. Seconds later he stood behind her, devouring her with his gaze. He took in every silken inch of those endless, toned legs and swallowed at the promise of what lay hidden between them.

He trailed a finger between the curves of her butt, feathering it down over her pussy, and just as he suspected, he found her folds were hot, slippery and wet.

"Will is a friend. We met about eight months ago. Waved at each other through our windows." Ben knew Melissa deserved to hear the full story, especially after discovering Will had seen them last night. What Ben hadn't expected was *wanting* to share such a personal piece of his life with her. "He's a decent guy. Not bad looking, or so I've been told. A little taller than me. In his early thirties. Blond hair, blue eyes. A soccer player in his spare time. And the thing is..." He hesitated for a heartbeat. "Will and I? We like to share women. Like to fuck them...at the same time."

A jolt went through Melissa, and this time Ben knew it wasn't an orgasm. It was shock. "W-what did you say?"

"You need me to repeat it?"

She didn't turn around, didn't look at him. "In detail!"

"Hand me your vibe first."

Melissa didn't move.

"Well, okay, then." Ben gave a nonchalant shrug and slapped her lightly on her rump, enjoying their power play. "No worries. Get yourself dressed, and I guess I'll see you tomorrow?"

He might sound as if he didn't care, but his stomach twisted at the thought of her pushing her skirt back down and walking away. They'd come too far to end things now. Ben wasn't ready to let her go.

With a soft whimper, Melissa relented. She grabbed the toy and handed it to him.

Vibrators sure had come a long way since the Rabbit. This one looked like an elegant sculpture one might want to display on a mantelpiece. It quivered to life with a soft hum. "Nice."

Ben let the toy vibrate over her buttocks.

"Tell me about Will."

Like he'd done with his finger earlier, Ben trailed the vibe between her butt cheeks over her delectable-looking hole and lower. He settled the tip at the very spot where her juices glistened between her lips.

Melissa gasped.

"Will likes to watch. Likes to see a woman take her pleasure before he gets involved."

Melissa groaned and clenched her pussy lips, relaxed them, clenched them again and twisted her hips, as though trying to take the vibe in deeper.

Ben refused her the satisfaction. He held it where it was, the tip teasing her wet opening. Her reaction to the gentle torment was a heady aphrodisiac. Blood pounded in his temple. In his cock.

"Play with your clit, sweetness, and I'll give you what you want."

"S-sweetness?"

"It's more affectionate than Mel. And watching you squirm like this? Watching your pussy begging for more? It's bringing up all sorts of affectionate feelings inside me." Nope, the shy blush that had reddened her cheeks last night was the real reason he'd thought to call her sweetness.

With a strangled sob, Melissa spread her legs wider and moved her hand between her thighs. He couldn't see much, but from the way her pussy pulsed, he knew she'd found her clit. He inched the tip of the vibe inside her and was gratified by the way her hips bucked in response.

"Tell me more about Will."

"Ah, yes. Will." He couldn't resist the sight of her arse any longer. With his free hand, he traced a fingertip lightly around her hole and was rewarded with a low hiss. "I bumped into him one day as I left the office. Said hi. We started chatting, went for a drink. He's an okay guy. We got to be mates after that."

Will had invited Ben to join his soccer team, and Ben had accepted gratefully. It had felt good to make friends again. To build up a social life.

"One night, while we were having a laugh, a woman walked into the pub. A good-looking woman." For the first time in a very long time, he'd found himself attracted to someone other than his ex-fiancée.

"Describe her." Melissa's legs trembled.

"Tall, with dark, shoulder-length hair, big breasts and eyes that said *dare me*. Sitting there, watching her, made me hard."

"You got an erection in a pub?"

"I did." Ben almost shook his head in disbelief. The story was getting Melissa even hotter. Goose bumps covered her skin, and her pussy dripped.

"D-did *he* notice?"

"Will?"

"Yeah."

"He noticed *her*. The woman. Told me, and I quote, 'I'd like to take that fine arse home with me for the night.'"

"What did you say?"

"I warned him he'd have to take me home with her, because I'd seen her first and I wasn't about to give her up for him. He laughed, and joked about sharing her."

"D-did you laugh?"

"Not once."

The suggestion had knocked him for a loop.

He'd had a threesome before, with Sienna. He'd shared her with another man. And the experience had been...profoundly fucked-up. While he'd loved the kinkiness of a ménage, and while the sex had been unbelievably good, the psychological consequences of what he'd allowed to happen had screwed with his head for months after.

It still screwed with his head.

He'd shared the woman he'd loved with another man. Allowed someone else to touch her while he did. How could he have ever let that happen? How could he have ever thought that would be okay?

"You took him seriously?"

"Very seriously." Much to Ben's surprise, Will's suggestion had appealed to no end.

Because while he'd hated having another man in bed with himself and Sienna, he'd gotten into the sex act with three people. He'd found a release and excitement in it that he'd never had with just one partner. And the thought of doing it again, that time with a woman he did not love, well, for some reason, it had been irresistible.

"The thought was just as big a turn-on as the woman was. Just considering the idea of having sex with her at the same time Will did got me almost as aroused as I am right now. Almost."

Fact was, he couldn't remember ever being as horny with

anyone as he was with Melissa.

Melissa inhaled audibly. "You're turned on right now?"

It was his turn to growl. "I'm so fucking hard I could come just watching you touch yourself."

"A-are you hard for me? Or for the woman in the pub?"

There it was. That hint of insecurity in her voice. No matter how confident Melissa might act, she still had doubts.

The question was, was she doubting herself, or him? "The woman in the pub is a memory, sweetness. Nothing more. You..." Ben squeezed his eyes tight. Well, hell. What could he say now? *You make me want more than a quick fuck and a fast orgasm? You make me long for the days when I believed in love, when I believed that being a part of a couple was the happiest way to exist?* "You make me burn." His voice came out hoarse and raspy. "I wanna fuck you so bad I can't stand it."

She whimpered—a sound Ben was beginning to associate with an instant rush of blood to his groin.

"Did you fuck her? The woman in the bar?"

"I did."

"Were you and she alone?"

He waited a heartbeat. "No."

"Will was with you."

"He was."

"Did he watch?" A shiver raced through her.

"You mean like he watched us last night?"

Her answer was a throaty yes, punctuated by a visible tremor through her body.

"He did."

"A-and she didn't mind?"

"Oh, no, sweetness. She didn't mind one bit." She'd thrived

under the attention of two men, relished it. So had Ben. But only sexually. Emotionally it had wrenched his gut, made his chest hurt and forced him to relive his night with Josh and Sienna all over again.

"Will didn't...participate? He only watched?"

"He participated."

"Specifics!" Melissa demanded.

"Okay, specifics. I fucked her and Will watched, then Will fucked her while I recovered. Then we both fucked her. At the same time."

Melissa moaned. And Ben couldn't resist the temptation of her gleaming pussy any longer. He slid the vibe all the way inside her, as deep as it would go. Then he clicked a button, increasing the speed.

Melissa cried out, her relief and desire reflected in the sound.

Ben ate up the sight of her back arching, her hips twisting. He filled his ears with the sounds of her sensual cries.

Long seconds passed before Melissa spoke again, and when she did, her voice was throaty, sexy. "Did you...enjoy it? Fucking her at the same time as he did?"

Did he? The physical gratification had been undeniable. The excitement, the pleasure, the release, the relief...he'd gotten out of it exactly what he thought he would, a couple of good orgasms—exactly what he'd needed at the time.

But neither of those orgasms had given him the emotional gratification he'd ached for. The emotional gratification Mel had given him last night—before she'd clammed up on him.

Easier not to answer, he decided. Easier to divert the question. "Are you enjoying this? My story?"

"I... Oh!" She twisted her hips again, whimpered. "It's

making me...burn."

Her choice of wording was not lost on Ben.

"Making me want to...come."

"Again?" Ben kept his voice stern, needing nothing more than to see her explode. See pleasure take over her body and her mind. "Haven't you already come tonight?"

"O-only once," Melissa complained. "Not enough."

Not enough for him either. Not even close to enough. He clicked the button again, increased the vibe's speed. Melissa's moan was low, feral. Her arm shook. The same arm she used to touch her clit.

"Wanna know the crazy thing, Mel?"

"Mm. Wanna know everything 'bout you."

She did? Wow. He inched closer to her, wrapped an arm around her waist and replaced her finger with his, thrumming her clit. "The sex with her was good. It was hot. But..." He blanked. Couldn't remember what he'd meant to say. Mel really wanted to know everything about him?

"But?"

"But no matter how many times I came with her—not one of those orgasms compares with the orgasm you gave me last night."

Melissa froze. "I-it was that good?"

Her shyness and uncertainty tapped at his heart. Did she even have to ask? He leaned over and placed a kiss on her spine, right between her two shoulder blades. "Sweetness, that was the best sex of my life."

Chapter Five

Melissa scratched at the windowsill, sought desperately to find purchase, find something to hold on to, something to keep her upright.

Pleasure, extreme and absolute, swept over her. Ben had had the best sex of his life—with her.

God, she was close to coming. So close. She couldn't ever remember being this aroused, this stimulated, this frantic for more.

More, more, more.

More of Ben.

More of the bliss he gave her, the carnal, wanton, wicked euphoria he bestowed upon her.

She wasn't earthbound anymore. Wasn't a solid mass. She was floating on air. A million light years away from the office. She was in heaven. In paradise, languishing in a cloud of undiluted ecstasy. She was an empty, aching vessel, desperate for fulfillment. Desperate for the release only Ben could give her.

Ben stood behind her, doing incomprehensible things. Naughty things. Wicked things. Making her crazy. Making her insane. The idea that someone had seen them last night was a potent aphrodisiac. Hearing Ben speak about a threesome he'd had? Outrageous that it should turn her on so. But it did.

God, no wonder she was losing touch with reality.

Handfuls of heaven usually weren't given to her. Not like

this.

But here they were, she and Ben. Ben confessing he'd enjoyed being with her. More than enjoyed.

She'd fantasized about him a million times but never dreamed the reality would be better than the fantasy. So much better. And yet his hands, his kisses, his adulation... Oh, God!

Good, so unbelievably good. Her body burned, rocketed past the boiling point. She needed to come. Wanted the release. Melissa closed her eyes and pressed her cheek against the cool glass of the window, the cold a striking contrast to the heat of Ben's touch.

Hot, cold. Finger, vibe. Pleasure, need. He had her balancing on such a tight string she feared she might topple over any second.

And then Ben did the unthinkable. He pulled away, removing the vibe from her pussy. He left her there, empty, shaking, sobbing, a fragmented bundle of billions of aching nerve endings.

"Noooo," she howled. *Don't go. Never go. Never leave me.*

She didn't want to be alone anymore. Didn't want to live the life she'd chosen, the life she'd paved for herself. The life that left no room for anyone else.

She should go after him, chase him, bring him back, make him the one to share her life, but her legs wouldn't move. They were locked in place by an overabundance of pleasure and need.

"Ben!" She called his name, begged him.

"Right behind you, sweetness."

And just like that a pair of hands wrapped around her hips, legs pressed close to hers, and something hard brushed the sensitized lips of her pussy.

Hard. God, so gloriously hard.

It didn't vibrate. Not even a little bit, but with one clean thrust, that something hard filled her. Filled her, stretched her and delighted her like the toy would never have been able to.

Ben.

She tried to call his name, but was incapable of making sound. Incapable of doing anything but experiencing the very heights of rapture. The vibe was arousing. Satisfying. A huge turn-on. But Ben. Oh, God, Ben was perfect. Ben took her to new heights, heights she'd previously thought impossible to scale. Ben standing behind her, thrusting into her. A real, live male, muscles pulsing, heat pouring off him.

He smelled so good. Like spice and man and sex.

Or maybe it was her who smelled like sex.

It didn't matter. She inhaled huge gasps of sex-tinted air, giving herself over to the mind-blowing pleasure that was all Ben Cowley, relishing it, basking in the heat.

This wasn't just sex. Melissa knew that she could never have given her body so completely to a man she felt nothing for. A man she didn't trust. She trusted Ben. And she liked him. So damn much. She always had, she'd just never let him know.

So engulfed was she in her pleasure and thoughts, it took a moment to realize the sounds he'd made had turned from guttural moans to actual words. He was speaking to her.

"...see it? Are you okay with it?"

See what? Okay with what?

Her brain couldn't make sense of his questions. It was too absorbed in the physical reaction of her body to his.

"...light... Office. Stop...you want to."

Stop? This? Sex? Nooooo. Never, Melissa never wanted to stop making love to Ben.

But she didn't have a choice. Ben thrust once more, filled her, then ceased moving, his cock a solid, enticing, unmoving presence in her cunt.

"*Noooo*," she complained out loud.

"He's watching us, sweetness. Looking straight through the window."

Melissa straightened, yanking her cheek away from the cool glass and snapping her head around. Finally she understood what Ben was trying to tell her.

A soft light flared in the office opposite Ben's. The dim glow outlined vague details of a desk and a chair. Someone sat in the chair. More than that Melissa could not determine.

All she knew was she stood before the window with Ben behind her, fucking her. And somebody—Will—watched them.

"Ben?" Her question was whispered.

"He's there, sweetness. He can see everything."

Shock took her breath away. "M-my jacket is wide open. He can see my breasts." It was one thing imagining what she'd do if she was being watched, another thing altogether to know someone was actually there.

"He can." Ben hesitated, letting the knowledge settle in her mind. "Does that bother you?"

Did it? "I...I don't know." Her nipples grew tighter, but Melissa was unsure whether that was from horror—or excitement.

Ben shifted behind her, pulling her upright, the action bringing his cock more snugly inside her pussy and his chest closer to her back. It sent tiny ripples of pleasure undulating through her. His hands left her hips and snuck around her jacket, finding her breasts, palming them. Hiding them from the watchful gaze of the man opposite her.

"Better?" he whispered.

Was it?

She didn't know.

She loved—*loved*—the feel of Ben's hands on her breasts, holding them, cupping them. She loved it more that as soon as Ben heard her uncertainty, he raced to cover her up. Raced to protect her from the stranger's gaze. The windowsill and wall hid her lower body, and his hands concealed her breasts.

She'd been absolutely right to believe she could trust him.

On the other hand, she couldn't deny the disappointment that washed through her, knowing his—Will's—view had been blocked.

"We could stop this now, Mel," Ben soothed. "End the game by closing the blinds. Or I could step away and you could pull down your skirt, get dressed." He buried his nose in her hair, and a warm waft of air tickled through the strands and over her neck.

Options. The man was giving her choices. Letting her decide what to do, where to take it from here.

"Or," he whispered, and the mere sound of his voice sent a hot thrill through her, "I could fuck you, just like this, at the window, knowing he's watching." He punctuated this option with a small twist of his hips, withdrawing from her ever so slightly and then plunging back in.

At this angle, she doubted he could move any more freely, and that was fine with her. The thrust was hard, intimate. Ben was close. So close his chest pressed against her back, his heat warming her even through her jacket—although his legs no longer touched hers. She suspected he'd had to bend his knees to accommodate the change in position.

As minute as the action had been, Melissa felt it all the way down to her toes, the resonating echo of pleasure pulsating in every muscle.

She fixed her gaze on the man in the chair, couldn't seem to look away. Didn't want to.

"Fuck me," she said. "Just like this." As she voiced the words, she realized this was exactly what she wanted. Ben, inside her, making love to her. Ben, so close she could inhale the same air he breathed. Ben, fucking her, while his friend watched. "Don't stop. Please, don't stop. Ever. I couldn't bear it. Need more. Need...you."

Ben was moving. Pulling back and thrusting into her, fucking her in the confined space they had available. Twisting his hips and plunging his cock inside her, filling her with indescribable pleasure.

His hands clamped around her breasts, holding her upper body immobile. Her hips were pinned between the windowsill and Ben. She couldn't move, could barely inhale enough air to keep her lungs oxygenated. Or perhaps the lack of air came from the fact she'd forgotten to breathe, forgotten to do anything but luxuriate in the magnificent bliss Ben wrought on her.

It lasted hours, or perhaps only seconds. All Melissa knew was the rhapsody and the torment building, the pleasure climbing towards a peak. Part of her gloried in the thrill of being watched, in the wickedness of knowing they had a voyeur. She and Ben were not alone in this steamy, lascivious act.

Will was there too, observing every action.

Funny that she'd let him watch, let him see so much. Funny that it had such a dizzying effect on her. How bizarre that a stranger could have such an intimate view of this sexual side of her and yet know nothing about her thoughts or feelings.

Ben shifted them, moving his hands. One arm banded across her breasts, concealing them from view, and his other hand slipped low, resting against the mound of her pussy.

Where before the windowsill and wall had hidden her from the waist down, now Ben pulled her backwards a step, allowing Will a view of everything.

Or did he?

Ben's hand covered her pussy, and from such a distance, Melissa knew Will wouldn't be able to see that she'd shaved herself bare—for Ben. He wouldn't be able to see the way Ben's finger slipped, unhindered, over her clit. Or the way Ben slid it ever so lightly against that swollen bud, up and down, round and round, teasing, caressing, stroking, just like he stroked into her from behind, thrusting, plunging, driving. Deep, deeper.

Melissa tried to keep her eyes open, tried to watch Will, see his response. It was a useless exercise. Her lids closed. She had neither the strength nor the inclination to leave them open. She leaned into Ben, accepting his support, glorying in it. Pressure built inside her, a combination of the erotic tease of his fingers and the carnal thrusting of his cock.

She couldn't breathe. No longer needed to. No longer needed anything but Ben. Melissa screamed as her orgasm broke. The pleasure was too intense, the build-up too powerful. She couldn't contain the sound, couldn't hold back the force of the climax as it hit. Waves crashed down in bursts of sheer bliss, consuming her, overwhelming her.

"*Mel.*" The agonized cry told her Ben was right with her, his own climax taking hold of him. Every muscle in his body turned rigid. Even the finger on her clit stopped moving, although he kept it there, kept up the pressure so every time she shuddered she jerked against the finger, prolonging her release.

As her pussy convulsed around him, grabbing him, holding

him, his cock pulsed inside her, over and over, his climax as interminable as her own. God, was it as good for him, as satisfying? As mind-blowing? Could anything be as good as this?

"Mel, ah, fuck. *Mel.*" The raw passion in his voice sent shudders cascading through her. Ben called her name. *Hers.*

As the last tremors of their spent passion rolled through them, Ben released her from the strong grip he held her in. He didn't let her go, didn't expose her to Will. He simply loosened his hold, letting her breathe freely. But he stayed pressed against her back, his heat pouring into her, his breath echoing in her ears.

And she stayed right where she was, content for him to hold her weight, to give her strength.

Eons later, Ben slipped out of her pussy. He eased her skirt back over her hips and then, one arm still concealing her breasts, leaned sideways and pulled on the cord of the blind.

Just like that, Will was locked out of the room.

"Some things are not for his eyes," he whispered. He took a couple of seconds to dispose of the used condom, then he spun Melissa around, wrapped his arms around her and caught her mouth in an intoxicating kiss. A kiss that lasted forever. A kiss that made her already shaky knees weak and her already pounding heart race.

A kiss that she could not have pulled away from had a hurricane blown over them. A kiss that sealed Melissa's fate. No matter where their affair went from here, and no matter what he thought about it, she was his. Her heart now belonged to Ben.

Damn it. She'd never meant to lose her heart to him. Never meant to get emotionally involved. She couldn't afford the luxury. If she fell for Ben, she'd focus on him instead of work.

She'd lose track of her goals, and she'd never become partner. Which would make one more notch in her belt of failures.

Mel may have lost her heart to Ben, but she hadn't lost her head. She knew what she had to do now. Shift walls to hide her true feelings from him.

Ben lounged at her office door as Melissa turned her back and donned her shirt. She'd returned to professional mode, had already brushed off his touch as he reached to straighten a stray strand of hair.

"Honestly, I don't need an escort," she told him. "I walk to my car alone every night of my life."

Frustration prickled his spine. She'd just opened up and given him everything. Why did she have to close him out so quickly? "I'm not escorting you, Mel. We're parked in the same car park, I thought we could walk there together. It makes sense."

"I'd feel more comfortable if we left the office separately." She packed her briefcase, neatly and efficiently.

"Why? You think someone will see us together and suspect something is going on?"

Her cheeks flushed, and her hands stilled, then she unpacked and repacked her entire briefcase.

Hello again, shy and uncertain Melissa. At least she hadn't gone AWOL. Ben would have missed her.

"That's exactly what I think," she said.

"Sweetness, we've already been seen together."

Panic crossed her face. "Please tell me you know him well enough to assume he won't say a word?"

The need to protect her rose in his chest. "He won't." Ben

had absolute confidence in that. Neither he nor Will was the type to kiss and tell. Or watch and tell, for that matter.

"Good." Her sigh of relief was audible. "I wouldn't like anyone else aware of what's going on between us."

Okay, taking precautions to ensure no one walked in on them while they had sex was one thing, but this bordered on neurosis. "And two colleagues walking out of an office together is going to tell the world what? That we're lovers?"

She blinked.

"I'll be walking beside you, Melissa, not fucking you on the footpath."

Her face flushed and for a second she had a wicked gleam in her eyes.

"Oh, fuck." Ben took a shuddery breath. "You'd like that, wouldn't you?"

She shook her head. "What I'd like is irrelevant. I'm just acting the way I feel I have to in public."

He refused to do this. Refused to let her push him away. Melissa was not a nameless woman he'd shared with Will. She was a lover he was fast becoming addicted to.

"Fine." Ben shrugged, pretending she didn't frustrate the hell out of him. He'd try a different tack, one he knew she wouldn't ignore. "I thought I could take the opportunity to tell you about my phone call with Everton this afternoon, but I guess it can wait 'til tomorrow."

Melissa eyed him warily but finally conceded with a nod. She closed her briefcase, stepped past him and walked out into the corridor. Why, oh why did she feel the need to keep her distance? Did he scare her? Bore her? Threaten her?

He wanted to reach out and grab her hand so he could hold it in his. Or put his arm around her shoulder and pull her close to his side, keeping her there. He wanted to take her home with him, strip her naked and make love to her for the rest of the night. Or for half the night, at least—and spend the remainder of the dark hours curled up around her slumbering body.

He gave in to one instinct, reaching out to take her hand.

For a few moments she let her palm rest against his, even tangled their fingers together. Her hand felt warm. It fit perfectly against his.

But when the doors to the lift slid open, she pulled away.

As the lift descended to the ground floor, Melissa cleared her throat. "So, what did Everton say?"

"He said yes. They're going to issue the debt. We need documentation on their desks by four p.m. tomorrow."

"Took them long enough to make up their minds, but at least we've got them on board."

Ben nodded. "You have the paperwork ready?"

"I do. We'll go through it first thing in the morning, make sure everything's in order and courier it over."

"As long as we do it in your office, that's good for me."

Melissa raised an eyebrow in question.

He repressed a grin. She may have reverted to full-on professional mode, but he hadn't. "We could do it in my office, but just know that if we do, the minute the last I is dotted and the final T crossed, I am going to strip you naked, throw you over my desk and fuck you 'til you scream. And I don't particularly care who sees us."

"Ben, I beg you. Restrict talk like that to your office, after hours. Where no one but you and I can hear it. Please."

The doors opened, and Melissa all but raced out of the lift into the deserted lobby.

Ben had no compunction calling after her, knowing his

words would stop her in her tracks. "Why are you running, Mel? Because you don't want me to fuck you on my desk, in broad daylight, when everyone can see? Or because you do?"

She skidded to a halt and slowly turned to face him. "I'm not running." She looked oh-so calm, but the frantic pulse beating in her neck gave her away. "I made my intentions clear last night. We work, we fuck, we go home. Whatever happens between you and I happens in your office. Period. Outside of your office, we are work colleagues, nothing more."

"That's bullshit. We're out of my office now, and we're a whole lot more than work colleagues. Deny it all you want, but that's the plain truth. Hell, Alistair is a work colleague. I have no desire to push him against the wall and fuck him six ways to Sunday. You, on the other hand…" He took a deep breath. "You I'd take in a heartbeat, if you just gave me a sign." He pointed. "Right over there. Against that wall."

Melissa turned to look at the wall, licking her lips nervously, gratifying Ben to no end.

"The only reason I'm not pushing the issue right now is because I left the condoms in my desk upstairs."

"Ben—" Melissa spluttered. Fury darkened her eyes. Fury and desire. "I refuse to discuss this further."

"And I refuse to talk about work after what just happened between us."

"Fine, then we won't talk. I didn't want to talk in the first place. I didn't even want to walk outside with you."

"That's a lie, Mel, and you know it. You want to be with me. You just don't want anyone to be aware of it."

She turned and marched off. He fell into step beside her.

"Why?"

"Why what?"

"Why won't you be seen in public with me?"

"I've already told you."

They exited the building, jogged down the stairs and hit the footpath, both of them taking a right towards the car park. "And I've already told you that excuse doesn't cut it. Do I embarrass you? Scare you, maybe?"

"What? Don't be ridiculous."

"Hardly ridiculous when you won't acknowledge my existence outside of my office."

"Of course I acknowledge your existence. We work together."

"We don't have to just work together. We could actually be—" he clutched his heart dramatically and gasped, "—friends."

Melissa almost tripped but righted herself just in time. She shrugged off Ben's steadying hand. "I don't want friends. I've already told you that. I want to make partner. I don't have time for a social life."

"Partner or not, we all need friends. Life's too short and too lonely to go without." Man, had he ever learned that lesson from experience.

"I'm doing just fine without, thank you very much."

Melissa wouldn't look at him.

"Are you? Really? You're reduced to fucking a colleague in an office when the rest of the company has gone home. Is that what you want? Emotionless sex to tide you over until you make partner? And then what? Socially, your life is going to be perfect all of a sudden? Because you've succeeded in your business goals, you'll miraculously have a life?"

She turned to glare at him, but anger was not the only emotion he saw on her face. Hurt and pain framed her ire. It made Ben want to take her in his arms and hold her. Hug her. Protect her. Make everything better.

"Making partner is my life, Cowley. Sex with you is a...fringe benefit."

Ouch! "Ah, so now I'm a fringe benefit. Nice."

"I never gave you any reason to think you would be more." No, she hadn't, had she? And yet there'd been moments, several of them, when they'd connected on a level that hadn't been purely sexual. Or purely professional. And it was those moments that gave him reason to want more from her.

"You never gave me reason to believe you wanted to fuck me either, until you stripped naked in my office."

Melissa shrugged. "What can I say? I'm full of surprises."

She looked so controlled, looked so together, but Ben suspected she was anything but. He suspected that beneath that distant veneer was a lonely woman screaming out for company. For friends. Maybe even for love.

They reached the car park and for the second time in a few minutes climbed into a lift. Ben did nothing, leaving it to Melissa to push the required button.

"Surprise me now. Have lunch with me tomorrow."

She shook her head and furrowed her brow, looking worried. "I'll have sex with you tomorrow night. More than that, I draw the line."

"You have a deal. On the sex front. As for the lunch—I insist. It's not a date. We can call it a business lunch. Hit the coffee shop on the ground floor. After all, you were the one who pointed out I miss too many lunches. C'mon, sweetness, help me correct that now."

"Don't call me that." She stepped out of the lift and took a left. Ben followed. The level was all but deserted, just one car parked on the other end. A black Peugeot Cabriolet. Nifty little car. Racy. Nothing like he'd expected her to drive.

On second thought, having met the other side of Melissa, maybe the Peugeot was the perfect car for her.

"Don't call you sweetness? Sorry. No can do. Now that I've had a couple of tastes of you, I know it to be the truth. Can't call you anything else."

"Back off, Cowley."

"Tell you what. Forget going out to lunch. I'll bring sandwiches to you. We can eat in your office. Or mine. But if we eat in mine, you know I'm going to have to have dessert." His mouth watered at the thought.

She clicked the remote for her car, and her indicator light flashed. Faster than he'd anticipated, her door was open and she was seated in the front, the keys in the ignition. Ben crouched next to her before she could slam the door shut.

"No sandwiches," she informed him. "No lunch. No socializing. No nothing. You and me, we're about work and we're about sex. And that's it."

Ben frowned at her. "I'm confused. I thought you wanted me to be happy."

She gaped at him.

"Your words. You said that. Last night."

"When I offered you sex. I figured that would make you happy."

"It did. It does. But I'd be happier spending time with you. Not talking about sex. Or work." He screwed up his nose. "Nope, cut that. We can definitely talk about sex. And other stuff too."

Melissa sighed. "Please, let's not turn this into something it's not. I can't afford to be distracted now. Too much is at stake if I lose my focus. We're sex, Ben. That's all."

Hell, she was closed and unapproachable. Nothing like the wanton sex goddess who wanted to know everything about him not half an hour ago. "Are we sex now?"

"No, we're colleagues now. Period." She didn't look at him when she answered. Her expression was stoic, unemotional. But she shifted just the tiniest bit in her seat, and that was all Ben needed.

He placed a hand on her knee, letting his fingers inch under her skirt. "So if I moved my arm up your leg, let my hand trail over your inner thigh, I wouldn't find you wet and wanting?"

Her cheeks turned scarlet. "You wouldn't find me anything, because your arm is not moving another inch."

Too late. He'd already let his fingers whisper up her thigh, already lost himself to the heady feel of silk and heat.

"Ben—"

"Have to touch you, Mel."

"Leave me alone!" Her command was a hoarse whisper.

"Open up for me, sweetness." The fog of desire quickened his breath.

"No. Please, go away." But her body's response contradicted her words. She parted her legs for him.

"That's it." His hand crept up over her smooth skin. "A little wider."

She slumped against the back of the seat, spreading her thighs as far as her skirt would let her, allowing him in. It was a tight fit but worth the effort. He found her exactly as he'd hoped to. Wet and warm. Slick with desire.

"Mel, you're killing me."

Her response was a soft moan.

He couldn't resist drawing his finger through all that heat, from her swollen pussy lips up over her clit and back down again. She shuddered at his touch.

"You feel so good." Ben closed his eyes, let his hand and her soft whimpers lead him. "So fucking good. You make me want to do wicked things to you. All night long." He played with her bud, rubbing it gently, listened to her labored breathing.

His ankles burned as they held his weight, and the muscles in his legs bunched and began to cramp, but he refused to move an inch. All he wanted now was to taste another one of her addictive kisses. "Lean in close, sweetness. Give me your mouth."

He opened his eyes in time to see her roll her head to the side so she faced him. Her eyes were dark with desire, her lips parted.

"Closer." His mouth was parched, desperate for a sip of her.

She inched closer. He lifted to meet her. And then her mouth was on his, and he drank from it deeply. Her lips, soft against his, her tongue, velvet warmth, her taste...intoxicating.

Mmmm.

He dipped a finger inside her, angling it just so to compensate for her sitting position, and knew in that moment, that just as Melissa had claimed she wanted to know everything about him, he wanted to know everything about her. Every single thing. From what she looked like nude to what drove her so hard to succeed. And as erotic and sexy as slipping his finger in her pussy while she sat in her car was, more than anything, he wanted to take her home, lay her on his bed and make love to her. Unhindered. Unwatched. Just him and her.

Her restless sigh and the clenching of her inner walls told him she was close. Very close.

Ben did the very thing he knew she'd hate. He withdrew his finger.

79

She moaned her dissatisfaction into his mouth.

He pulled away from her lips.

"Noooo."

He clenched his hand into a fist so as not to give in to what they both wanted him to do. "Have lunch with me tomorrow."

She swiveled her head from side to side. "Touch me."

"Sandwiches in your office. That's all."

Her face was flushed. "You're a bastard."

"I'm not. I'm a real nice guy. Have lunch with me so I can prove it to you."

"I don't want lunch."

"Honestly? I don't either. It's the conversation I'm after. Personal conversation. About you, not work."

"Why do you have to make this personal? Why can't we just keep it physical?"

"Because physical isn't enough for me. I need more from you than just sex."

She looked at him with big, uncertain eyes. "The...the sex isn't good enough?"

"The sex is amazing," he rushed to assure her. "I just want more from you than amazing sex."

She twisted in her seat and whimpered. "I've given you my body. What more is there?"

"There's a whole person in there I'd like to get to know."

Melissa glared at him.

He swiped a finger over her clit, reminding her what she was bargaining for.

Her entire body bucked. "Fine. Lunch. But that's all."

"That's all for now, anyway." He couldn't contain his satisfied smile. Nor could he hold back another second. He gave

80

her his finger, rewarding her wholeheartedly for her decision. As he slid the digit inside her, he stroked the pad of his thumb over her clit.

Melissa stopped breathing.

Had the door been closed, steam would likely have misted the windows. The sounds of her pleasure filled the car, echoed through his ears, and then she was coming. Clasping his finger inside her, holding it, releasing it, the velvety walls of her pussy clenching rhythmically.

When she collapsed against her seat, spent, he pulled his hand away, brought his finger to his mouth and licked it clean, tasting her passion all over again.

A powerful shudder rocked her body as she watched him.

Ben cast her a smug smile as he stood up, stretching the kinks from his legs. "See you at lunch, sweetness."

He leaned in, planted a kiss on her luscious lips and walked off to find his own car, parked three levels up from hers.

Chapter Six

Melissa eyed the sandwich. "Thank you, but I'm lactose intolerant. I can't eat cheese." How had she let him talk her into this? What had she been thinking when she'd agreed to lunch?

"You are?" Ben looked surprised. "Funny, you never mentioned that before."

"There's a lot I never mentioned to you before." Grumpy. That's what she was. Grumpy and unimpressed. Not with Ben, mind you. With herself, for giving in to him so easily. She found it almost impossible to feel unimpressed with Ben.

"Not just to me. Thought you might have mentioned it in all those business meetings we've had. You know, the ones where you quite happily accepted any cappuccino ever offered?"

She glowered at him. Duh. Of course he'd seen her consume milk before. "Fine. I'm not allergic to milk. I'm allergic to you."

He settled himself in the chair opposite hers with the desk between them. A veritable feast was spread in front of her.

He raised an eyebrow. "Did you break out in a nasty skin rash? You know, after what we did last night."

"As a matter of fact I did." She scratched her forearm for emphasis.

"Ah, the classic post-coital itch." He tut-tutted. "Nope, sorry. I've seen it before, and it's not me you're allergic to. It's the vibrator. You might wanna try a different one next time."

Damn it, the man was incorrigible. He wouldn't let her win

this. Ben was hell-bound and determined to have lunch with her and to make conversation. "I thought this lunch was going to be about me, not sex."

"You're the one who brought up the post-coital itch."

"Huh!" She folded her arms over her chest. "I did not. I merely mentioned being allergic to you."

Ben leaned forward and whispered conspiratorially. "You know, sweetness, when your skin flushes red and your breasts and pussy swell, it's not allergies. It's arousal. Big difference."

Melissa shook her head, at a loss for words.

Ben relaxed back into his chair. "And in case you're interested? I'm suffering from a similar affliction right now. Although, to be honest, I'd never mistake it for allergies. This is one itch I'd really like to scratch."

Her mouth twitched into a smile. How could it not? "Could you just eat your food and stop talking?"

He selected a beef sandwich on Turkish bread smothered in mustard and took a healthy bite.

"Let's try this," Melissa suggested. "Let's see how long we can go without mentioning sex. I give you five minutes, tops." Herself, she gave about half a minute. But then what living female wouldn't think about sex when sitting opposite Ben Cowley?

"Is that a challenge?"

She shrugged. "Take it however you'd like."

"Challenge accepted. Okay, let's see. Work talk is out, sex talk is out. What else can we discuss?"

Melissa helped herself to a container of fresh yogurt topped with sliced mango and passion fruit. It was her favorite. "The weather?"

"A possibility." Ben nodded. "Or you could tell me about

83

your drive to succeed. The need to make partner."

Sheesh, the man didn't beat around the bush. He drove straight to the heart of the matter. "Why is it so important you know?"

"Because I was once like that. Driven by the same determination that pushes you." He hesitated. "It cost me the woman I loved."

His confession took her by surprise, and her gaze shot to his face. "Sienna left you because you were dedicated to your work?"

"Sienna left me because I dedicated my life to my job instead of my fiancée."

Wow. Okay. She hadn't known that. "You're worried I'll dedicate my life to my work instead of my fiancé? Newsflash, I don't have a fiancé." Although once she'd come close. Once. A long time ago.

"Yeah, and have you stopped to wonder why?"

"I don't need to wonder why. I don't want a fiancé. I want to succeed in business." Or perhaps it was more a case of she *needed* to succeed.

"You have succeeded, Mel. You're brilliant at what you do. I've never seen anyone better. But does your job keep you warm at night? Does it give you someone to go home to? To keep you company?"

She didn't like his questions. Not one bit. They hit a nerve somewhere deep inside and threw her off balance. "You know what you're doing, don't you?"

"Enlighten me."

"You're transferring your issues onto me. Making your problems mine. They're not. We're different, you and I. Have different reasons for doing things. I don't have a Sienna in my life because I don't want one." She had wanted one, once upon a time.

"Then tell me what you do want. No, wait. I know what you want. Tell me why it's so important for you to succeed."

Some things were too personal too talk about. Too hard. "It's none of your business."

"You made it my business when you seduced me. When you drew lines around the boundaries of our relationship. When you told me you wanted me for some things but not others. I'm only human. I can't see those boundaries as clearly as you can. If you want me to respect your wishes and your needs, help me see them clearly. Give me a reason to keep my distance."

She so didn't want to go here. So didn't want to talk about this. But she guessed she owed Ben a little insight into the way her mind worked. She wasn't that cold and callous that she could fuck him and then refuse to speak to him. Was she?

"Okay. If it's so important, I'll try to explain." But she needed to do it in terms he could understand. "Tell me something first, though. Tell me how you felt when you realized you'd lost Sienna for good, when you realized she was never coming back."

Ben's jaw tightened. "Why? It has no bearing on your reasons for working so hard."

Ah-ha. So she wasn't the only one who struggled to discuss the real, personal issues. The ones that cut deep. "Maybe not, but it'll help you understand what motivates me."

"Fine." Ben dropped his gaze to the table, but not before Melissa saw a wealth of pain in his eyes. "I was gutted. Felt like a train had ridden over me, every wheel of every carriage leaving its lasting mark."

The hollowness in his voice broke her heart. "Did...did you try convince her otherwise? Convince her not to go?"

"I changed my life trying to convince her," he ground out. "Cut down my work hours by a quarter, changed my work contract. I gave up the very thing that had chased her away in the first place—my complete and utter dedication to my job. But I was too late. My efforts failed. Miserably."

"I'm sorry, Ben. So very sorry for your pain."

He shrugged. "It wasn't your fault."

"I know that, but it doesn't mean I can't sense how deeply you're hurting." Dredging up his pain wasn't her intention, but his answer provided the common link Melissa had sought. The common bond that would help Ben understand what drove her to be the best. "You see, I understand failure. All too well. I've failed too. A few times. And it's..." She hesitated, chewed her bottom lip, wondered how much to say. "It's destroyed me. Destroyed my life. Broken me and left me with nothing." Wow. Okay. She hadn't expected to say that much. Not even close.

"Go on," Ben urged.

"It's, uh, I... It's the fear of ever falling so far or so hard again that makes me so desperate to succeed. That's why I have to achieve every goal I set for myself. That's why I can't let anything interfere with those goals. It's why I'm determined to be the best I can be at whatever I undertake."

Ben's gaze was on her, intense, probing. "It's hard to imagine you've ever botched anything. From where I'm sitting you look nothing like a failure. Nothing at all."

"I'm glad that's how you see me. I want everyone to see me like that. I never want anyone to know just how badly I've screwed up in my past." Dear God. What was she saying, spouting her mouth off like this?

She'd just confessed something about herself to Ben she'd never told another living soul. Not her mother or father or even any of her sisters.

"What happened, Mel? What hurt so bad it's turned you into the woman you are today?"

Melissa took a deep breath and forced back the words that popped into her mouth. The truth. Some things were just too hard to talk about, and she'd already divulged way too much information.

He gave her a sheepish grin. "Okay. That was a tough question. Too tough. Let's start with an easier one. You said you've failed a few times. What's the least important failure? The one that hasn't changed your life, but you're still keenly aware of?"

Melissa took her time, studying her hands as she helped herself to a few more spoons of yogurt.

Ah. Right there. A perfect example for Ben.

She held up a hand to him. "There you go."

Ben stared at her, perplexed. "Your hand?"

"No, my fingernails. Look at them."

Ben looked and still remained perplexed.

"I'm a nail-biter. Have been since I was three years old."

"Uh. Okay." He sounded uncertain. "So what?"

"My mother did everything in her power to stop me from biting them. Everything. Sent me to school with Band-Aids on every finger, put some foul-tasting polish on my nails, punished me every time she found a finger in my mouth. Even tried a star chart system, rewarding me if I went a week without biting." She stared at her fingers. "I never did get a single reward out of that chart."

"So you're unsuccessful because you bite your nails?" He looked at her as if she were crazy.

"My mother would say so."

"Would you?"

"I'd like longer nails. Prettier nails." But on the scale of all she wished she could achieve, beautiful nails were not high up there. She chuckled at his baffled face. "You asked for my least-important failure. I'm showing you."

"And I appreciate that confidence. Thank you."

"You think I'm mad."

"Nope. Not at all. We all have things we wish we could change about ourselves but never get around to doing."

Melissa sighed. "I had a ton of things like that growing up."

"Like what?"

She looked at him warily.

"The unimportant ones, Mel. The ones you don't mind talking about."

She thought about it for a while. "Well, I was a terrible netball player. Always wished I was better, but I just never quite made the team, no matter how many times I tried."

"So you tried, knowing you were no good?"

She nodded.

"That must have taken a lot of courage."

"Some, I guess. Or just sheer stupidity. But after being knocked back continually, I stopped trying."

"We all would," Ben said.

"I guess." She breathed deeply. "I was a God-awful dancer too. Never could make it up on my toes, much to the despair of my ballet teacher."

"Did you enjoy ballet?"

"Hated it, with a passion. But my mother was a dancer, and all three of my sisters too, and I didn't want to disappoint them." With that disclosure, Ben knew more about her family and her past than anyone else at work did. How on earth had she admitted so much about herself to him?

"Did you disappoint them?"

"My mother, maybe. My sisters never cared whether I danced or not."

"I have a confession to make," Ben told her then. He lowered his voice, as though afraid anyone would hear them through the closed door. "I was never much of a dancer either. Never once made it up on my toes."

"Did you try?" Melissa asked, startled by the thought Ben may have done ballet.

"Er, hell, no. Why would anyone try something they hated?"

She looked at him, felt her lips twitch again. "Touché, Mr. Cowley. Point made." She tilted her head to the side, watched him. "But I didn't hate debating. I loved that. Disappointed my school horribly, though, when I agreed with the opposition. They kicked me off the team."

Ben snorted. "You didn't."

"I most definitely did."

"Okay, then, that I concede is a failure." Not that he looked horrified by it. Not in the least.

But then Melissa didn't want him horrified. She just wanted him to gain some understanding as to why it was so important she work so hard now. Work so hard to the exclusion of everything else in her life.

"There were more, Ben. Other, more significant failures that I can't speak about. But that's why I'm so determined now. I've failed once too often in my life. It's ruined me. I don't ever want it to happen again."

Ben regarded her with serious eyes. "We can't all be good at everything."

"You're right. We can't. But there are some things we have

89

to achieve. Some things that define where we go from that point on. And if we don't achieve them, life changes in ways we never expected or never wanted." And that was as much as she would tell him.

Ben must have picked up her resistance to carry this conversation any further. He regarded her in silence for a long while. "I hope that one day you'll trust me enough to tell me about the failure that changed your life."

She shrugged. "Perhaps one day." She left it at that, noncommittal one way or the other.

He pushed a paper plate towards her. "You haven't eaten enough. Try this."

Melissa stared longingly at the treat in front of her. Sweet pastry wrapped around decadent caramel and smothered in milk chocolate. A billion or so delicious calories just waiting to be eaten. Begging to be eaten. With a will of iron, she refrained from grabbing it and shoving it into her mouth.

"It's a caramel kiss," Ben said. "My weakness. I have to have one a day. At least."

"I know what it is," Melissa answered demurely, feeling anything but. The only thing that tempted her more than the dessert was the man sitting opposite her. "But I can't eat that."

Ben raised a teasing eyebrow. "Another allergy?"

"No, dummy. Another kilo heading straight to my hips."

He *ts*k*ed*. "Trust me on this. You have no problem with your weight. None whatsoever."

"Hah. Tell my mother that." The woman had been on her back since she was ten, harping on at her about her too-large behind and her overly rounded hips. Melissa's obsessive need to run every morning did not stem from a love of the exercise. Although now she found if she didn't run every morning, she didn't have as much energy as usual. Truth was, the runs had become kind of addictive.

"I'm telling *you*. A caramel kiss is not going to do you any harm. Eat it." His voice brooked no argument.

She gazed longingly at the treat.

"Okay, I'll give you a choice. One way or another you get a kiss this lunchtime. Either take a bite of the dessert, or I'm going to plant my lips on that luscious mouth of yours and kiss you. With tongue. Lots of tongue. In broad daylight, while the entire company is at work." He shrugged. "I know which one I'd prefer, but as I said, the choice is yours."

Melissa couldn't help it. She licked her lips.

Ben growled low in his throat. "Choose. Now."

She grabbed the caramel kiss and took a bite. Sensational sweetness burst in her mouth, making her moan out loud. God, that tasted good.

"Lucky pastry," Ben muttered. His eyes were black as night. Desire glowed from them.

Melissa chewed and swallowed, then held the kiss out. "Help yourself."

Ben did not take his gaze off her mouth. "I intend to. Tonight. I intend to help myself to every last inch of you."

She looked pointedly at her watch and grinned in triumph. "Twenty minutes without a mention of sex. That's fifteen more minutes than I gave you credit for."

His smile was hungry. Predatory. "Give me those fifteen minutes tonight and then see what you can give me credit for."

For once Melissa did not bother to adopt her stern, professional demeanor. "And if I don't restrict you to fifteen minutes?"

Ben studied her for a long, charged moment. The air

between them seemed to vibrate, awareness and lust growing quickly. "Then hopefully I can gain a lot more credit in your eyes."

She smiled at him. If he gained any more credit in her eyes, she'd have to put him on a pedestal. "I'm looking forward to you trying."

He smiled back. "Not as much as I am, sweetness."

lapsed onto the couch. "Come here, sweetness." He
arms to her.

me, slowly and hesitantly, but she came. And when
out and placed one of her hands in his, he tugged
ll into his lap. This time when he kissed her, he
top the tenderness that had overwhelmed him from
ugh as their mouths met.

was exquisite. And determined. And shy. And all
e had a lifetime of failures that plagued her, failures
't let defeat her. What she didn't have was a man to
d to look after her.

served to be adored.

t his lips relaxed and his tongue gentle as he kissed
she kissed him back in just the same manner.
nderly. Deeply. Intimately.

previous kisses had been exciting, passionate and

as all that, yet so much more.

tretched out on the couch, taking Melissa with him.
l her body close to his, so close they could have been
still it wasn't close enough. He wanted—no, he
be inside her.

she whispered, as though reading his thoughts.
to me."

oked into her eyes and nodded his agreement. Any
onse would have sounded glib.

y on his back, with Melissa straddling his hips. As
ey'd been making love for a lifetime, she lowered
to him as he thrust his hips up. Their joining was

lid inside her wet, waiting warmth.

Chapter Seven

Ten o'clock could not come fast enough for Ben. Blessedly, the offices emptied well before the allotted time. By eight thirty, he and Melissa were the only two employees on the floor.

Which meant he had an hour and a half of torturous waiting before he could hold her again. If the minutes had passed slowly last night, time seemed to stand still tonight. Ben swore his watch stopped at 8:37.

Need and lust and want prickled every inch of his flesh. His skin pulled taut over his joints, making movement painful. He was in hell. He had become an aching body of desire, every thought centered on Melissa, every breath.

If Melissa had thought she could deter him with her stories of failing, she'd been wrong. Hearing she had faults and weaknesses only endeared her more to him. Only made her more human.

By nine o'clock, Ben could stand it no longer. It might be an hour too early, and he might be breaking yet another of Melissa's crazy rules, but he didn't care. The need to see her again, taste her—hold her, talk to her—was too strong.

He marched across the two corridors it took to get to her office.

There she was, her hair caught in a ponytail behind her head, her eyes trained on her computer screen, oblivious to his presence.

Ben crossed the office in a couple of steps. Even as she looked up in surprise, his hands were on her waist, and he was pulling her upright. He hauled her out of her chair, straight into his arms, and before she had a chance to protest, crushed his mouth to hers.

For the first time since leaving her at lunch, Ben felt a measure of relief.

Finally, *finally*, he had her where he wanted her. And she was right where she wanted to be too, if the intensity of her kiss was anything to go by.

When had he become addicted to her? When had his need for her reached fever pitch? Why was she the only thing that could calm the restless twitch that had plagued him since lunchtime? Hell, since he'd left her in her car last night?

The need to undress her, to have her naked before him, wrestled with the need to hold her.

He settled for stripping her, one item of clothing at a time, without ever releasing her lips. Sweet. She tasted so damn sweet. Like the caramel kiss she'd consumed earlier. His favorite treat. His weakness.

Her hands were as busy as his, tugging at his tie, tearing at his buttons, yanking at his zip. The soft, hungry whimpers she emitted sent blood racing to his cock, and by the time she pushed his pants and boxers over his hips, he had a raging erection. Again.

Who could blame him? He held a bare Melissa in his arms. Every inch of her silken, nude flesh was pressed against his naked skin, from her toned thighs to the flat plain of her belly and the gentle swell of her breasts.

Closer. Christ, he wanted her closer.

She released his mouth just long enough to murmur the word *couch*, and then their lips were melded together again. Several moments passed before they made it to sofa on the other side of her office.

Tonight Ben knew there w

His need for her was too great.

hips against his, he suspected s

Ben pulled away, but only

pants pocket, and then she wa

considered laying her down on t

changed his mind.

"Tonight, I get to watch yo

tangled his hands in her hair. H

gorgeous tresses loose. Prim and

their lovemaking. He wanted the

She helped him, tugging a

elastic, and there it was. Her mar

her shoulders, framing her face.

His breath caught. "Well, hell

She caught her lower li

uncertainty crept into her huge, h

Ben shook his head, awed by

his throat. She was a bit of alright.

She blinked, startled. "I am?"

"You take my breath away." H

air to fill his lungs.

Mel smiled shyly at him, a smi

he'd tried to coax out of her just a

the confident, seductive looks sh

nights, the disparity hit him full in

This was the other side of Meli

even. A side that hid the confidenc

her. It touched something deep insi

hadn't expected to be touched ever

him.

Ben co

held out hi

She ca

she reache

until she

could not

coming th

Meliss

woman. S

she would

love her a

She d

He ke

her. And

Sweetly. T

Their

sexy.

This

Ben

He presse

one, yet

needed—

"Ben

"Make lo

He l

vocal res

He

though

herself o

seamless

Ben

When he was seated to the hilt, they both stilled and looked into each other's eyes. Words were unnecessary. Melissa leaned down and offered him her mouth.

He took it, in a greedy kiss that lasted a lifetime. A kiss that rocked him to his very soul. Lying on the couch with Melissa above him, surrounding him with her heat, something clicked inside Ben. Like the changing of gears. Like he'd been driving in second gear for the last nine months, grinding aimlessly uphill, and had finally hit a flat and effortlessly changed to third.

The change was right. Easy. And so steeped in emotion Ben could not begin to figure out what exactly had changed. He just held on for the ride.

And what a ride. When Melissa drew away from his mouth, her lips kiss-swollen and her eyes closed, oxygen again eluded Ben.

She wasn't just beautiful. She was a goddess. Perfect.

She lifted her torso up and began to sway atop him, the slick heat of her pussy pulling at his erection, consuming it, then releasing it in a sensual rhythm before consuming it all over again.

She danced above him; the long, elegant lines of her body epitomizing all that was feminine. Her breasts swayed as she moved, their seductive tempo hypnotic, and he couldn't look away.

Ben let her lead him, losing himself inside her. He held her slim waist, his hands absorbing the satiny smoothness of her skin, and wondered again how he could have been so oblivious to her hidden beauty—both physical and emotional.

As much as Ben would have loved her dance to last forever, the tightening in his groin told him he wasn't going to last much longer. Impossible to hold back the orgasm that built inside him. She was too appealing. Too irresistible. She made him feel...too much. Real, honest emotion he hadn't felt since Sienna. Different emotion, but real nevertheless. Powerful.

Her neck was flushed, her nipples beaded, and she'd tunneled her fingers into her hair, thrown her head back and closed her eyes. The expression on her face was a mirror of the pleasure he experienced. Her sultry lips had parted, and blood tinged her cheeks pink.

He couldn't resist her swaying breasts, raising his hands to cup them both, filling his palms with their soft weight. Her nipples stabbed at him, making him impossibly harder, and Melissa sighed a sultry sigh.

Absolute beauty.

His hips were moving now, driving his cock into her as she danced. Driving it deeper. Hell, he couldn't get deep enough. Yet pleasure suffused his veins, his lungs. His heart.

It was Melissa who ratcheted up the ante. Melissa who changed the game. She dropped a hand to her pussy and stroked her clit.

It was too much, sensory overload.

"Mel..." He couldn't speak, couldn't find his voice.

She stroked faster, began to bounce on him, took him in as deep as he needed to be inside her. The flush on her neck swept down to encompass her chest, and just when Ben established he could not last another minute, another second, Melissa came.

She arched her back above him, thrust her breasts hard into his hands and dissolved.

The walls of her pussy clenched around him, tightening, relaxing, tightening, relaxing, so fast, Ben was once again lost to the rapture of their lovemaking.

He let her orgasm guide his own, and then he too was coming. Convulsing below her, shuddering, his cock pulsing inside her. It wasn't like the previous orgasms with her. Not quite so frantic, frenzied.

This one was slower in building, yet far more powerful. This one involved not just a physical release, but an emotional one as well. As he came, he let go of his past.

She'd done it. She'd freed him from the shackles of his pain, of his hurt. She'd given him this incredible gift.

For the second time in his life, Ben learned what it was like to come inside a woman he'd begun to care deeply about. Sex with Will and their women was just that. Sex. But with Melissa, he cared. And that care made this orgasm all the more meaningful. All the more pleasurable.

All the more about Melissa.

Mel.

His sweetness.

Tonight she didn't resist when he tried to walk her to her car. She didn't even attempt to walk ahead of him or three steps to the right. Tonight they walked together, side by side the entire way. And when they reached her car and Ben tugged her into his arms and kissed her goodnight, she did not pull away. Regardless of the fact that the car park was half full, and people milled about around them, she kissed him right back.

A sweet, intoxicating kiss, the perfect complement to the sweet, intoxicating love they'd just made.

And when she climbed into her car and waved goodbye, Ben cursed the weekend that stretched empty ahead of him, void of her presence.

On Sunday morning he gave in to his impulses and phoned her. He half suspected she wouldn't answer. Not only was he breaking all her golden rules about keeping their professional relationship professional and their personal relationship about sex and only sex, he was phoning her, on her work mobile, on the weekend.

He didn't care. He'd missed her. Saturday night had been cold without her. Dull. At nine forty-five, he'd almost left Will and his mates at the pub and headed to the office. Just in case.

Common sense had kept him where he was. Melissa would not be working. Even he knew that any open deals she had on her table were as up to date as they could be. She couldn't find more work to do, no matter how driven she was.

He'd declined Will's subtle invitation to a threesome. The other man had nodded towards a woman surrounded by her friends and raised an eyebrow. Ben had answered with a shake of his head—and ignored Will's knowing smile. A threesome was not what he wanted. Melissa was.

Neither of them mentioned Will's late-night observations at the office. Neither needed to.

By nine o'clock the following morning, Ben couldn't hold back any longer. He lay in his big, empty bed and thought about Melissa. He thought some more about her, and a little more after that. And then he grabbed his phone, found her number and dialed, expecting the call to ring through to voicemail.

Her throaty, "Melissa Sparks speaking," undid him. His semihard cock flared to life again at the sound of her voice.

"Hey, Mel."

A brief hesitation. "Ben?"

"Yeah, sweetness. It's me."

"Is everything okay?"

"Everything's fine."

"Uh, then why are you phoning?"

"No reason. Just wanted to hear your voice."

"Ben—"

"I miss you."

"This is highly inappropriate," she huffed.

Ah, there was the Melissa he knew and loved. Not. "Wanna hear something even more inappropriate? I fell asleep last night thinking about you, Mel."

"Melissa," she corrected, just like he knew she would. "And no, I don't want to hear that."

He grinned and palmed his cock. "Would you rather hear that I woke up thinking about you?"

"No. Definitely not."

"I also woke up with an erection."

A heartbeat passed before she responded, but in that heartbeat, Ben heard it: a whisper-soft whimper. "Don't do this, Ben."

"Don't do what?"

"Make it personal."

"Too late, sweetness. It's already personal. When I wake up with a hard-on and you on my mind, you better believe it's personal."

She sighed into the phone. "Do you still have it?" Her sternness was gone, replaced by a kind of grudging acceptance.

"My erection?"

"Yeah."

"I do."

Another whimper.

Ben stroked his cock. "I've had it since I woke up. Haven't been able to get out of bed because of it."

"So...so you're lying in bed, talking to me, with an erection?"

"Correction. I'm lying in bed, naked and talking to you, with an erection."

She waited a moment. "I'm lying in bed too."

"Naked?" He closed his eyes, imagining her as such and stroked a little faster.

"No." Another soft sigh. "I'm wearing knickers."

"Nothing else?"

"Nothing else."

He squeezed his eyes tight. "Take them off, sweetness."

"Why?"

"Because I want you to touch yourself while you talk to me. That's why."

"Oh." She sounded contemplative. "Okay."

He swallowed a groan.

For a good few seconds only her breathing and the rustle of something in the background echoed through the phone. And then, "Done."

"They're off?" he asked.

"They're off," she confirmed.

"Where's your hand?"

"Honestly?"

"Honestly."

"On my breast. Squeezing it."

"I'd like to put my hand on your breast."

"I'd like you to put your hand on your cock."

"It's already there."

A small intake of breath. "It is?"

"I've been stroking it since I heard your voice."

"My voice is that big a turn-on?"

"*You're* that big a turn on."

"Keep talking, Cowley."

"Touch your pussy, sweetness."

"I...am."

Ben shuddered. "Good. Now tell me how it feels."

"Sensitive," she replied. "Warm. And... *Oh!*" A soft gasp. "...Wet." Her voice was a good three tones lower than it had been.

"Where are your fingers?" Hell, he wanted every detail.

"One is on my clit. Rubbing. Another is...*mmmm*, sliding...inside my...*ahhh*...cunt."

Ben stilled. He hadn't expected her to answer her phone, he hadn't expected her to talk to him, and he sure hadn't expected her to indulge in dirty talk. It made his dick swell even further. "Your wet cunt?" Forming words in this state was harder than he'd thought it would be.

"My v-very wet cunt."

"Good. Keep it there. Keep sliding it in and out while you play with your clit."

"Tell me about your erection."

"It's big. Almost as big as it was on your couch. And hard. So hard it kind of hurts to touch it."

"But you are touching it?"

"Can't stop," he confessed. "And knowing where your hand is now? Don't wanna stop."

"Mmmm. Me neither."

Silence filtered over the phone as he stroked himself, imagining her hand on her pussy. He stroked a little harder. Moaned.

Her answering groan lit his stomach with fire.

"Tell me about your weekend." Where he found the energy to talk, he had no idea, but he just wanted to hear her voice. Wanted to know that although they weren't together, they were right there on the same wavelength.

"It was okay. Quiet, I guess. Yours?"

"Okay. Lonely." Now why did he admit to that?

"You been alone all weekend?"

"Nope. I was out last night with some mates." He tugged harder on his dick. "With Will."

Silence greeted him. Silence that extended for too long.

And then, "Did...did you and he...?"

"No." He released his cock and sat up, hearing something he couldn't identify in her voice. "No, sweetness. We didn't."

"Why not?"

Why not, indeed. He grabbed his erection again, resumed stroking it. "Because I wasn't interested." True. For the first time since he and Will had shared their first woman, he had no interest in sharing another one with his friend.

"I, er, thought it turned you on?" Her voice was hoarse. And curious.

"It does. It just didn't turn me on this weekend. You did."

"You never saw me this weekend."

"I know. And I wish I had. I've been in a state of semipermanent arousal since Friday night."

Her breath whispered over the phone. "M-me too."

"Christ, Mel." He couldn't finish what he wanted to say. If he did, he'd beg her to come round, and every instinct he possessed told him that would be a mistake. She'd refuse. He had her now. On the phone. He had her fingers in her pussy, and although it wasn't him doing the fucking, knowing she was fucking herself more than sufficed—for now.

He changed the subject, moved to less volatile ground. "What did you do this weekend?

"Went to a movie. With my sister."

"Which sister?"

"The one who's a year older than me."

"Do you see her a lot?"

"Yeah. She's my best friend."

"You're lucky. To have siblings. I don't have any."

"I am lucky. They're good sisters. All of them."

"Do they know you seduced me at work?"

"What? God, no!"

"If they did know, would they approve?"

It took a while for her to answer. "If they knew it made me happy, they'd approve."

He smiled, immediately liking her sisters. They'd approve for the right reasons. "Did it make you happy?"

She didn't answer.

"Where are your fingers now, sweetness?"

"Where are yours?"

"Wrapped around my cock. Still."

"Mine are in my pussy, still. Well, one is. One's on my clit."

"Did seducing me make you happy?"

"Yes. It did."

His heart stuttered. "It made me happy too." Before he let the moment and the admission overwhelm them, he launched into another question. "Ever had a finger in your arse?"

She answered without skipping a beat. "Not my finger, no."

"So, someone else's?"

Her silence was all the answer he needed.

"Did you like it?"

When she responded her voice was tinged with the same shyness he'd seen in her smile. "A lot."

He lowered his voice as he powered his hand over his erection. Precome spilled from his tip, lubricating his palm. "Ever had a cock in your arse?"

There it was. Another whimper. "Are you offering yours?"

It took a good few seconds before he could answer. "Yeah, sweetness. I am."

"In that case...I accept."

A deep groan escaped from his chest. "Fuck, you're hell-bent on killing me with lust, aren't you?"

She laughed throatily into the phone. "You asked."

"I did." Another groan. "And now I can't wait."

"Me...neither."

"Mel?"

"Yeah?"

"I'm gonna come." His orgasm pounded in his tight testicles.

"Now?"

"In about ten seconds."

A whimper. "Let me hear it. Every bit of it."

"'Kay." He spasmed. Once. Groaned. Grabbed the base of his cock as his orgasm hit. "Oh, *fuck!*" It slammed through him. "*Fu-uck!*"

Every muscle in his body tensed as come shot through his dick, pulsing out of him. "C-coming, sweetness." A string of semen landed on his stomach. "Coming...hard." Another one landed just below it. "*Ahhh.*" Another pulse, another string of semen. "*Mel!*"

Her cries echoed over the phone as he called her name.

She was coming too. Coming in time with him. Calling out his name, whimpering. And then moaning wordlessly.

His dick pulsed again as he emptied himself all over his belly. Even after the come ran out, he dry heaved, pulsing in time to her moans, breathing heavily. And then not breathing at all.

He collapsed onto his back, utterly spent, listening to the sound of her ragged breathing. When at last it had slowed to a pace he thought she might be able to talk, he growled into the phone.

"Sweetness?"

"Hmmm?"

"Tomorrow night, your arse is mine."

Chapter Eight

True to his word, on Monday night, Ben made her arse his. And it felt so damn good, Melissa offered it again on Tuesday night. And Wednesday. On Wednesday night, it felt even better than it had the previous two nights, but that was probably because they weren't alone.

Will watched them.

And he made no bones about it either. He pulled up a seat at his window, and with the light beaming down on him, he sat and enjoyed the show, even giving her a thumbs-up when it was over.

Once again, Ben refused to let him see the good bits, or her naked bits at any rate, but it did not detract from her pleasure at all. She felt naughty and decadent and sexy and aroused all at once. And she loved every minute of it.

Or perhaps she loved every minute of being with Ben.

Ben.

He'd started phoning her first thing in the morning. Every morning. It was, Melissa decided, a very satisfying way to start the day. Way better than the run that followed the phone call. He also insisted on walking her to her car every night. And planting a very sexy, very thorough kiss on her mouth when he said goodbye. She'd stopped resisting. Couldn't see a reason to refuse his company and goodnight kiss anymore, especially because no one from their office had seen them together at the end of the day—yet.

He hadn't tried to bring her to orgasm in her car again, but then he didn't need to. By the time they left the office at night, Mel was so sexually sated, she did not need anything more. Well, not until the next morning, anyway.

The next morning she'd wake to find herself swamped in desire, and just as she'd start to think the desire would overwhelm her, the phone would ring. And then it was quite okay for the desire to overwhelm her. So long as Ben was equally overwhelmed.

Along with Friday, Melissa's period came, and she was almost grateful for the excuse. She wasn't sure she'd be able to resist if Ben insisted on seeing her over the weekend.

Ben insisted anyway, but Mel held her ground. Sex with Ben was one thing. A relationship with him that had nothing to do with sex was another thing altogether. Like this, she could keep telling herself it was physical and nothing more. If she removed sex from the equation, and they continued to have such a good time together, she'd know it was more. A lot more.

And a lot more would interfere with her goals. She couldn't let that happen.

Still, Ben phoned her on Saturday morning and evening. And Sunday morning. And not once did he bring up sex. On Saturday morning he phoned to tell her he'd woken up with a craving for a caramel kiss, and on Saturday evening, he described in great detail every bite of the kiss he'd found at the bakery around the corner.

Melissa awoke in the middle of the night with an unnatural longing for a kiss. Well, two kisses.

When the phone rang on Sunday morning, she complained to Ben—at length—about how he'd kept her up the whole night. He accepted her grumpy rumblings good-naturedly.

On Sunday evening, the phone didn't ring. The doorbell did. And there stood Ben, holding a white baker's box loaded to the brim with caramel kisses.

Melissa accepted the box gratefully and sent Ben on his way.

He headed straight to his car, only to return a minute later with a bottle of wine. Hard as she tried, she couldn't get him to leave. Okay, so she didn't try very hard, but she did insist at least once. Ben agreed to go—just as soon as she'd shared a caramel kiss with him. Four hours later, her belly full of dessert and wine, she finally kicked him out. He left with a smile. She closed the door behind him, mirroring that same smile.

As weekends went, it was a good one. Okay, it was the most enjoyable one she'd had in...years.

On Monday and Tuesday, Ben followed up their early morning phone calls with lunch in her office. And on Wednesday, Melissa followed up their early morning phone call with a frantic dash to his office.

With her hands full of files, three people on her heels and her heart racing like crazy, she stood outside Ben's door, calling out urgent instructions to the junior staff members who reported to her.

"Jerry, I want that report finished, printed and on my desk in an hour for review. Sue, get Everton's secretary on the phone and make an appointment for tomorrow morning. Don't let her make any excuses for him. Not one. And when you're finished, get Westpac on the phone and make sure the money's been transferred. Pete, I need every document Everton ever signed double-checked right now. Also, let Alistair know Ben and I are dealing with the fallout, and I'll get back to him in an hour with a game plan. Now move it. Go."

She watched, gratified as all three of them ran to carry through on her instructions, then turned, marched into Ben's office and closed the door behind her.

He sat behind his desk regarding her with a worried look. "Problems with the Everton deal?"

Melissa shook her head. "Not one." She dumped her load on his desk.

He narrowed his eyes, obviously concerned. "Didn't look that way to me."

"Good. Then it won't look that way to anyone else in the office." She returned to the door and locked it. Thank God the only window to Ben's office overlooked another building and not the corridor of their offices.

Ben sat up straight. "Care to tell me what's going on?"

"It'll be easier to show you."

As she crossed the room, she looked into Will's office. There he was, sitting at his desk. She smiled, once, and gave him not another thought.

"Show me what?" Ben swiveled his chair around to face her as she walked.

"This." She eased onto her knees in front of him, pushed his legs apart and shuffled in close.

"Mel..."

"See, it struck me this morning, that for everything you and I have done together, or done over the phone, there's one thing we haven't tried yet." She kept her gaze pinned to his as she spoke, watching his eyes grow black as night.

"There's an office full of people right on the other side of my door," Ben warned. But that was all he did. He didn't walk away. Or push her away. Or try and still her hands as she worked on his belt, button and zip. Nor did he try to hide his growing erection.

"And most of them are, at this moment, trying to sort out a nonexistent crisis."

"It's the middle of the day, sweetness. A long way away from ten o'clock." He lifted his arse up off the chair, so when she tugged on his pants and boxers, she met with no obstruction. His cock popped up to greet her watering mouth.

"Very good, Cowley." She nodded her approval and folded one hand around his balls and the other around his erection. "You worked that out so quickly. I can see you must have shined in your math classes at school."

"Sarcasm, Mel?"

"Desire, Cowley."

"For math?"

"For a taste of you."

His cock jerked in her hand. "Carry on speaking like this, and you won't just get a taste. You'll get a mouthful."

"Exactly what I'd hoped for."

A bead of moisture trickled from the slit of his cock. "Anyone could walk in."

"The door's locked."

"Anyone can hear."

"Stop speaking and there won't be anything to hear."

Ben shut up. And then groaned low in his throat as she took him into her mouth, one rigid inch at a time.

"Not gonna last, sweetness," he warned. "Been waiting almost a week to come inside you again."

She didn't answer. Couldn't. Not with her mouth as full as it was. She dove into the task at hand, giving it her everything.

It didn't take long. Minutes maybe, before Ben's moans filled her ears, before his hands clasped her head and held her face still while he thrust gently into her mouth.

She sensed the restraint in his movements. Knew he held

back, restricting his thrusts for fear of choking her.

She was having none of it. He'd given her everything sexually up until now, held back nothing. He'd wrought orgasms from her with his mouth and his hands and his cock. It was only fair she give him back just as much.

She opened her mouth wider, and the next time he thrust inside, she caught his dick and swallowed.

"Holy fucking hell."

His shout was gratifying, although Melissa feared for just a second it would attract attention.

Then he pulled back and thrust again, and she forgot about the attention and focused on his cock. On the way it slid further and further down her throat. On the way his flavor exploded over her taste buds, salty, musky. He tasted like pure, unadulterated man.

She focused on the way his low groans filled the office, and how his thrusts intensified. Focused on keeping her cheeks hollowed, sucking him when he drove in and caressing him as he pulled out.

"Gonna come, sweetness." He clutched her face tighter, thrust faster. His voice was hoarse, and when she peeked up at his face, his eyes were closed, his head thrown back.

She sucked harder.

"Love...coming inside you," he rasped. *"Ahh... Fuck!"*

The words stopped, just like that. His cock pulsed in her mouth. Once, twice, and a burst of slippery fluid slid down her throat. Then another. She held off while she could, letting his orgasm flow, letting the pleasure take him, but when come began to spill from her lips, and she had no choice, she swallowed. Once.

Ben cried out and jerked. Another burst of fluid filled her

mouth. God, she'd wanted a taste and he was providing her with a healthy one. A delicious one.

He pulsed once more in her mouth, and the rush of fluid trickled away to nothing. The next time she swallowed, he pulled away from her.

"Too...sensitive," he gasped as she let his cock go.

Melissa leaned back on her haunches and watched as he struggled to catch his breath.

He watched her right back. Watched her wipe her lips with her thumb and forefinger, scooping off any come that had slipped out while he exploded and then lick those same fingers clean.

"Ya did that in broad daylight," he commented raggedly.

"Appears so."

"With the entire office right on the other side of the door."

Melissa nodded. "I did."

"Know what I reckon, sweetness?" Ben's eyes were glazed, his chest heaving.

"Nope. Tell me." She licked her lips, tasted his cock again, his desire and his passion.

"I reckon I'm falling in love with you."

Melissa tried to respond. God help her, she tried. But she couldn't. She just sat where she was, speechless. Her mouth gaped open, and she stared at Ben.

"Nah, scratch that. I reckon I fell in love with you the first time you walked into my office and let your hair down." He nodded. "No doubt about it. That's the exact moment I fell in love with you."

Melissa hid in her office for the rest of the day. She took just enough time to rinse her mouth out and assure her staff the crisis had been resolved, then she hightailed it to the safety of her desk and chair.

Not that she got any work done. Work was about the last thing on her mind.

Ben loved her?

Her?

It wasn't possible. Men like Ben didn't fall in love with women like her. They respected her business acumen from afar, or enjoyed her body from up close, but that was as intimate as they got with her.

She didn't let them any closer. Knew she'd only fail them if she let them in.

Just like she'd failed Thomas—and herself—all those years ago. A shard of glass cut her from the inside. God, she didn't want to think about Thomas. Didn't want to go there.

She thought about Ben instead, but then remembered what he'd said and so thought about the weather. Or tried to, anyway. But it was too late. She'd jumbled up Thomas and Ben in her mind, and now she couldn't stop thinking of either of them. Couldn't stop remembering the disappointment in Thomas's expression, or fearing the disastrous way things would end with Ben.

Because they would end. No way could they continue to see each other now. The last thing she needed in her life was a man who loved her. One who would make demands on her time, distracting her from making partner.

The minutes dragged, the hours felt like days. She counted each one until she could escape the prison that her office had become. A hell she'd helped create. If she'd just left Ben alone she wouldn't be in this situation now.

At five thirty she promised herself that come six, she could escape. She'd get out of the city center, get as far away from Ben as she could go. Find safety somewhere else, perhaps with one of her sisters? Perhaps she could—

The door flew open, cutting off any further thought.

"Get your things, Mel. We're leaving."

Her heart slammed into her ribs. "Pardon?"

"I'm tired of you running. Tired of you pulling away every time I make some leeway with you. This time you don't have a choice. I'm not letting you run. So get your stuff, and let's go."

She glared at Ben. "I'm not going anywhere with you."

"Yep, you are. We're going to walk out of the building together, while it's still busy and everyone can see us, and we're going to go sit somewhere nice and quiet and talk this out."

"There is nothing to talk about. You crossed a line today, a line you should never have crossed, and that can only mean one thing. This..." she waved her hand between them, "...thing, affair, whatever it is, is over. You changed the rules, changed the game, and I'm afraid the new game doesn't suit me. So, while it's been fun—and it has been fun—it is now over."

"This game is so far from over it's a joke. Now either grab your things and walk calmly out of the office with me, or I'm going to pick you up and carry you out of here. And on the way, I *will* stop in reception and kiss you. On the mouth, with tongue, for everyone to see."

As he spoke, he stood straighter, showing her his full height and the impressive width of his chest and shoulders. Melissa knew, without a shadow of a doubt, he would have no physical trouble carrying through on his warning.

She turned her back on him. "Your threats don't scare me. I'm not the only one with a professional reputation to protect.

There is no way you'd carry through on them. Now, if you don't mind, I'd like you to leave."

"Damn it, Sparks. You're too fucking proud for your own good."

Before she knew what was happening, Ben had lifted her up and slung her over his shoulder like a sack of potatoes. A freaking sack of potatoes!

Instinct made her struggle. She slapped at his back and tried to kick him, hard, where she knew it would do the most damage, but he wedged an arm around her knees, held her legs in place and headed for the door.

Panic struck.

He was going to do this.

"No, Ben. Wait!" She tugged frantically at his shirt.

He paused.

"Okay, I'll come with you. But I'm going to walk out of the office—you're not going to carry me."

"Not just out of the office, sweetness. You're going to come with me to a restaurant, and we're going to talk."

Melissa shook her head fiercely.

Ben shrugged and took another step.

"Okay, okay, damn it." Damn the man. "Fine, I'll walk with you to the restaurant."

"And sit beside me in said restaurant while we talk."

"And sit beside you in said restaurant while we talk." She fumed in silence.

"Good." He slid her down the front of his body, letting her find her feet. But the set down was slow, and as she slid, he pressed her close against a bulge in his pants. When she stood on her own two legs, he didn't let her go. He kept her pinned against him.

She glared at him, staring daggers into his amused eyes. "You're enjoying this?"

"I had your arse in my face and your legs dangling around my cock. What's not to enjoy?"

"You're turned on." Her voice was laced with accusation.

"Course I am. Your body's pressed against mine, your perfume is making me crazy, and I'm in love with you. Who wouldn't be turned on under the circumstances?"

Oh, God. Who wouldn't be, indeed? Her own traitorous body was beginning to show all the signs of arousal. Racing heart, tight nipples, butterflies in her belly and more than a little stirring of arousal in her now-soaked cunt. "I'm starting to despise you, Ben Cowley."

"No." He shook his head. "I believe you're starting to feel the same way I do, and it frightens the hell out of you."

His words hit a nerve—a very real, very raw nerve—and she stepped back, instinct telling her to put a little distance between them. "If you want to go to a restaurant, we go now. Or not at all."

He released her, giving her the space she desperately needed. "You're good at avoiding talk about yourself and about issues that matter, you know that?"

"I'll get my bag and we can leave." She turned and gathered the few things she thought she'd need.

"I won't let you avoid what's going on between us, Mel."

Irritation got the better of her. "Fucking you stupid every night is hardly avoidance."

"It is, if you insist that's all we have—a few nights of stupid fucking. It's more than that. Way more, and we both know it."

"You're deluding yourself, Cowley."

"Nope, sweetness, for the first time in months I'm beginning to see my life clearly. And I have you to thank for it."

"Save your gratitude. I suspect that by the end of the evening, thankful is the last thing you'll be feeling towards me."

With that, Melissa stalked out of her office. Fearing Ben might throw her over his shoulder once again, she made sure to let him walk at her side the rest of the way. She pasted a serene, professional smile on her face, and the two of them left the building.

Chapter Nine

He led her through the streets, down along several blocks. Melissa walked in silence, refusing to say a word. He'd gotten her to join him by force; no way would she make this easy for him.

Ben reached over and took her hand, twining his fingers through hers.

She let him, refusing to make a scene on the footpath, but made no effort to tighten her grasp. She left her fingers limp in his and pretended his touch didn't make her burn. Pretended the way his thumb stroked over hers didn't send shivers up her arm.

Pretended she wasn't at all affected when he raised her hand to his mouth and pressed a kiss to it. She pretended he wasn't there at all.

Pretty impossible to do when she was acutely aware of his every breath, his every movement. Aware of his spicy aftershave that drifted into her path, and the heat he emitted that scorched her side.

"It's funny," he said, as he drew his mouth away from her hand. "Until you mentioned you bite your nails, I'd never have noticed."

She pursed her lips and ignored him.

"But today, when you came into my office, took my balls in your hand and my dick in your mouth, I thanked God you bite them. Long nails in those circumstances? Not a good thing."

Don't respond. Don't respond. Don't gasp. Don't blush. Don't whimper.

"I can still feel it, you know?" He leaned his head in close to hers. "Your warm fingers around my scrotum and your hot, wet mouth around my cock." His voice became hoarse. "Hell, sweetness, I've been reliving it the whole afternoon."

She swallowed hard. Damn him. And damn her traitorous body that shivered as he spoke.

She should never have been so reckless. Never have gone down on him at work in the middle of the day. She just hadn't been able to stop herself. Just like she wasn't able to stop herself now as she let her fingers curl around his and let his touch warm her chilled hand.

He led her into a tiny restaurant and requested a small table at the back of the dim room. Not once did he release her hand. He kept it clutched in his, his thumb stroking over hers.

When Ben asked what she wanted to eat, she shrugged. "I'm not hungry."

Then she sat in surprised silence as he proceeded to order her favorite dishes. Linguine in a red wine and cream sauce, Italian salad with extra cheese and olives on the side, baked mushrooms with parmesan to start and raspberry sorbet for desert. He ordered double of everything except the pasta, replacing it with veal Marsala for himself. And then he asked for a bottle of Chardonnay and two mineral waters.

When the waiter walked away, she stared at him. "Th-that's exactly what I would have ordered. How did you know?" She couldn't help but think of the mango and passion fruit yogurt he'd provided for her at lunch last week. And this week.

He shrugged. "We've shared enough business dinners with clients. I know what you like."

"You took note of what I ordered?"

He nodded. "Apparently."

"I thought you'd never noticed me before now."

"That's an outrageous statement," he scoffed. "I said it before. You're the finest investment banker I've ever seen. I've always been aware of you, always watched you, always learned from you."

He paused while the waiter brought their drinks, then took a sip of wine. "I just never knew before now that you had the ability to drive me into a frenzied sexual lather. Or that beneath your stern professional veneer is a beautiful and appealing woman who managed to capture my heart."

His words made her head whirl. He thought all of that about her?

"Let me in, Mel. Give me a chance."

She bit her lip. "I've let you in. I've let you closer than any other man in a very long time."

"The sex is good. It's freakishly good. And I'm…I'm stoked that you let me discover your sensual, sexy side. But it's not enough. I want more from you, sweetness. I don't just want the caramel kisses and wild orgasms. I want to understand the way you think, what drives you, what makes you laugh, what makes you cry. What failure hurt you so bad you're determined to make partner at the cost of a personal life?"

"I don't want to talk about it."

"I know you don't. But sometimes talking about the things that hurt us the most helps free us from that hurt."

The waiter brought their mushrooms.

She didn't take notice. Her attention was focused on a very sudden, very clear realization.

She owed Ben the truth. Owed him an explanation about why she had to pull away from him. Why she had to reject his love.

She squared her shoulders, fortifying her defenses. And when the waiter walked away, and Ben looked at her with his beautiful dark eyes and said, "Talk to me, please," she knew she could put it off no longer.

Taking a very deep breath, she confessed in the softest voice, "I failed my HSC."

Ben's eyes widened. "Your final year at school?" His surprise echoed across the table.

It was the surprise that got her back up, made her defensive.

She nodded. "Yep. My final year in school. You know, the one you need to pass, and pass well, if you have any intention of going to uni? *That* year in school." Humiliation overwhelmed her. She couldn't look him in the face, couldn't bear to see the pity and sympathy and shock that shone in his eyes. It was always the response she got. Always. And she hated it. Seeing it in Ben would be the ultimate in mortification.

Nevertheless, she could feel his gaze on her as he sat there, speechless.

"I failed every single subject. Every one." Unlike her sisters, who'd all graduated with distinction and been accepted into whichever uni courses they'd applied for. She was the only major disappointment to her parents.

"What happened?" At least the question held no surprise. Or judgment. Ben's voice rang with curiosity—and caring.

She inhaled shakily, reliving the crushing disappointment, remembering the way her world had collapsed around her.

She'd felt worthless and stupid, as though she'd been robbed of every last drop of joy, pride and dignity. And the worst part was, she'd had no one to blame but herself.

"I got involved with the wrong crowd. Decided smoking and drinking and ditching school were more fun than learning. Decided to enjoy my final year rather than throw my youth away on studying."

"Was it an enjoyable year?"

The question surprised her. No one had ever asked her that. They'd all been too busy lecturing her about the error of her ways. "It was okay, I guess. I had fun."

"You don't sound convinced."

"The fun memories are kind of eclipsed by the fallout afterward. By the consequences of my slacking off." By the stark realization of what her careless, carefree attitude had wrought. She'd ruined her life.

She cut into a mushroom, stabbed a piece with her fork and shoved it into her mouth. It might have been delicious, but she couldn't taste a thing. She ate the entire helping without tasting it.

Ben ate too, but more to humor her, she guessed, than because he was hungry.

"My parents warned me," she told him. "They said over and over that my studies would suffer if I carried on the way I had been. I ignored them." She tried to disassociate herself from the memories. Tried to repress the misery and devastation and hell she'd been through, hoping that if she relayed it to Ben in an expressionless voice, she wouldn't feel the wealth of hurt and disappointment all over again.

It didn't work. It hurt as much now as it had then. Embarrassed her as much. "Turns out they were right." And Melissa never let herself forget that. Every time she let her guard down and found herself becoming too relaxed about her job or her life or her attitude in general, she reminded herself about her year twelve results.

"Mel?"

"Yeah?"

"How on earth did you become an investment banker if you failed your final year at school?"

Ben had a number of degrees, in finance and business and accounting. He knew, firsthand, what was required academically to reach the point she had in business.

"The long way. First, I changed schools and redid my HSC." That had been the second-most humiliating experience of her life. Nothing could be worse than failing the year. "I passed the second time round, but not well enough to get into uni." By that stage, Melissa's determination had come to the forefront. The day she'd received her second round of HSC results, she'd decided she would never, ever allow herself the shame of failing again. She would not only succeed at whatever she undertook, she would be the best. She would get to the top of her game, and she would not make excuses. She'd made excuses not to work for a year, and look where that had gotten her.

Never again.

"So instead of uni I went to TAFE and worked my butt off there. I completed a bridging course in finance at the technical school and then transferred to the University of New South Wales."

He gave a low whistle. "Couldn't have been easy."

"It wasn't." She swallowed down a massive lump in her throat. "It was...lonely. Horrible and lonely." For a few seconds she struggled to speak, struggled to gain control of her emotions. Even now, so many years later, the isolation of that time surrounded her, making her keenly aware of just how miserable she'd been.

The sound of cutlery clanging against a dish echoed through her ears, and then Ben's hand was on hers, holding it,

125

supporting her.

Over the years, she'd become adept at protecting herself from the memories, at keeping the sadness at bay, but ever since she and Ben had started seeing each other, she'd found she couldn't harness her emotions as well as she'd once been able to.

She couldn't control her physical reaction to him, and it seemed her psychological barriers were crumbling as well. Her defenses were breaking down. Ben was getting through them.

"I lost all my friends in the process—which wasn't a bad thing, considering the crowd I'd hung out with—but I struggled to make new friends at my new school." She'd been too embarrassed by her results to put her heart into anything besides passing her HSC, which had led to a very isolated year. "TAFE was a lot friendlier, but by then I was so determined to do well in my studies, I didn't give too much of my time to a social life. Until—"

Melissa snapped her mouth shut, stunned by what she'd been about to reveal.

"Until?" Ben's voice was gentle.

She stared dismally at her plate.

"Sweetness, don't pull back now. Please. Talk to me."

Melissa shook her head.

"I'm beginning to understand. Beginning to get an idea of what's made you into the person you are today. But I need more. I need to know everything that hurt you so I can help you past it."

His thumb brushed over her hand, so softly Mel was astounded by the comfort she gleaned from the simple gesture.

She bit her lip and forced herself to look up and meet his gaze. "I fell in love." She'd met Thomas and everything had changed. For a while she'd had it all. Her studies, romance and even a cartload of friends. Thomas's mates had accepted her with open arms.

"And?" Ben pushed.

"And...I was happy. Happier than I'd been in forever. Thomas made me laugh. He made my world brighter, sexier. He gave me a reason to look forward to every day."

"So what happened?"

"My life was rich again. Full. We were talking about moving in together, discussing forever, you know? It was all going perfectly—until one of my professors called me aside after a lecture and warned me that my results had dropped steadily over the last semester. He said if I didn't buckle down and do some work, I'd fail his course." She swallowed. "The worst thing was, I hadn't even realized my work was suffering because of Thomas. I thought I'd managed to maintain my studies. But I was wrong." She took a long sip of water. "I broke up with him that night."

"There was no alternative? No other option?"

Melissa shook her head. "I'd made promises to myself, Ben. I'd vowed to succeed. And then, there I was, breaking all those promises." The whole incident had been a double whammy for her. First she'd failed to have a social life and maintain her grades, and then she'd failed to sustain a relationship with a guy she'd really loved. "I didn't have a choice. There was no way I could live through the humiliation again." Ending the relationship had crushed her heart and her spirits, and changed her forever. She'd always remember the look on Thomas's face as she'd spoken to him, always see the disappointment in his eyes. She'd forever know she'd failed him as a girlfriend.

From that day on, she'd understood she could never have it

all. She could never have love, happiness and success. For her, the three did not go hand in hand.

"It wasn't easy, but I did it because I was determined to prove to my parents I could pass any course I undertook. I didn't want to disillusion them all over again."

"Did they support you?"

"Financially. They paid for my studies, but only under the proviso that I passed. They told me the first course I failed, they'd stop paying." She couldn't blame them. She saw no point in throwing money away like that either. "I couldn't afford to fail."

"And now you have an MBA."

"And now I have an MBA."

"Interesting, that."

"What?"

"That you have a master's degree in business administration and yet you still think of yourself as a failure."

She glared at him. "You try bombing out in your final year of school and not feeling that way. You try breaking the heart of the only person you've ever loved and see what that does to you."

"I'm not underestimating how terrible either of those were for you." Ben frowned. "It must have been a fucking nightmare. But you got past it. Rose above it. Proved that you could take your failures and turn them into successes. I don't know anyone else who's ever done that."

Was that admiration in his voice? And in his eyes? "There's no dignity in failing, Ben. It scars you forever, no matter how much you might achieve afterwards. Besides, I may have achieved academically. But I failed dismally at my relationship. I never got past that one."

Ben would not be deterred. "You've achieved more than anyone else I know, and yet you refuse to give yourself credit for it. I think you're amazing."

Without her ever noticing, their starters had been removed and the main course set on the table. Melissa dug into her pasta, refusing to let the warmth and genuineness of Ben's comments find a place in her heart.

For some reason, she was suddenly starving. Confessing to one's past failures must build one's appetite.

Expecting the linguine to be as tasteless as the mushrooms, she was surprised when flavor burst in her mouth. "God, this is delicious." She tucked in, eating with vigor, stopping only when she realized Ben was watching her with a bemused smile on his face. "You're not eating?" His food was untouched.

"I'm enjoying watching you."

She quickly dropped her fork. "Do I have sauce all over my face?"

He shook his head. "No, sweetness. You have a sinful look on your face. And it's giving me the erection from hell."

She shook her head, barely able to believe her ears. "My eating is making you horny?"

"You need only breathe and I get horny. Watching you eat is just icing on the cake."

"Now I don't get it." She looked at him in amazement. "I just told you how I flunked out in school and how I failed at love, fucking up my life completely, and it doesn't deter you?" Her confession was supposed to make him run. Get the hell away from her and leave her in peace to succeed.

"You just told me how you overcame your shortcomings to become the successful businesswoman you are today. That's not a failure, in my book. It's a huge turn-on."

"You're nuts."

"I am. Nuts about you. And just because one relationship didn't work out for you, it doesn't mean none will. We all have failed relationships. My engagement bombed out dismally. That doesn't mean I don't want to start again, try something new. With you."

Unsure how to reply, Melissa returned her attention to her food, not stopping until her belly was full and she couldn't eat another bite. Ben ate too. It was only when she pushed her plate away that he picked up their conversation.

"You don't see them, do you? The remarkable achievements you've made."

She sighed. Okay, how could she explain this so Ben understood? "There's nothing remarkable about it. I did it to prove I could. After my first HSC results came out, I thought I'd never get a university degree, so I didn't stop until I had an MBA. I feared I'd never get a decent job or earn a respectable living, so I searched until I found Preston Elks and investment banking. I doubted I'd have the wherewithal to last in a job like this, and years later I'm still here. I want to make partner to prove to myself, to prove to my parents, to prove to the world that I can do it. To show everyone I'm not useless."

Ben had stilled. His attention was focused on her, his dark brown gaze probing. "So that's why you're so driven, so determined. It's not about what you *want*, it's about proving you can do it."

She shrugged. "I guess."

"How long did you spend studying?"

"Nine years. But the last two were part-time while I worked at Preston Elks."

"And you've been at Preston Elks how long?"

"Five years. Five and a half."

"So that's what? Twelve and a half years of your life spent proving to yourself that you can succeed?"

"I guess."

"Is this what you wanted for yourself? Years ago, before your HSC, when you thought about your future? Did you imagine you'd be an investment banker?"

Melissa snorted. "Hell, no. I imagined I'd be a movie star. Or a TV presenter. Or someone famous."

"And now? Is this the life you want to lead?"

"Do I want to be a movie star now? Er, no, Cowley, I kind of outgrew that fantasy."

"Do you want to be an investment banker?"

She blinked, realizing what he was asking. And she didn't want to answer. "It's what I worked towards being for years. What do you think?"

"What I think isn't important. You just told me you worked towards this point for twelve years to prove you could. You never once mentioned doing it because it was something you *wanted* to do." He stroked her hand so tenderly, the touch warmed her entire arm. "Is this what you want to be doing with your life?"

She still didn't want to answer. "No, it's not. Okay? It isn't something I used to lie in bed at night and fantasize about. It's not the job of my dreams." It never had been. "But it's a good job, and I'm good at it, and it earns me a good salary, so I have nothing to complain about. Nothing."

"I've never heard you complain. But wouldn't working in a job you dream about be more fulfilling, more satisfying?"

Damn it, why wouldn't he just let this go? Why'd he have to

keep drilling her with his all-too-insightful questions? Couldn't he just let her pretend that she worked in a job she loved? "You know, you ask questions you have no business asking."

"And you change the subject every time the questions get too personal."

"The questions were never supposed to get personal. You were supposed to be someone I could fuck without complications arising. Full stop. You weren't supposed to probe into my psyche and try to understand what drives me."

"And you were supposed to be a business colleague I could work with and walk away from at the end of the day. You weren't supposed to seduce me, and enchant me, and make me feel things I haven't felt about a woman other than my ex-fiancée in nine years." His chest rose and fell. "Seems neither of us is any good at sticking to our original game plan."

"So tell me, Cowley. Where do we go from here? Neither of us has got what we expected. What do we do now?"

He contemplated her question a long while before answering. "We do exactly what you haven't done for twelve and a half years. We do what you *want* to do. Not what you feel you have to do, but what you feel you'd like to do, for no other reason than because it'll make you happy."

"What if what I want to do now is walk away? Leave? Finish what we should never have started and pretend it never happened?" That was what she should want to do. Otherwise she'd never make partner. She'd give too much of her time to Ben, like she had with Thomas, and she'd begin the downward spiral into failure.

Ben regarded her with dark, brooding eyes. "If that's what you really want, then so be it. Walk away, Mel. Leave me here and go back to the life you've created for yourself. Forget about us, forget about this. Go make partner. But you just make damned sure that's what you really want. Make sure it's what'll make you happy. Because that is the only way I'm going to let you go. If I know you're heading out on a path you want to walk, not one you feel you have to in order to prove a point."

Mel didn't move. The very thought of walking away left a horrible sensation in the pit of her stomach. For the last week or two she'd been happier than she'd felt in years. She'd smiled and laughed and enjoyed life.

And she'd done that because of Ben.

If she walked away now, she walked away from all that joy.

"Is it a path that'll make you happy, Mel?"

She stared at him, hating the sharp, jabbing pains in her belly, hating the unpleasant sensations that came with knowing she should give up the one thing that made her smile.

Finally she shook her head. "No." There was no way she would be happy if she left Ben.

"So choose another path. Do it now. For the first time in twelve and a half years, make a decision that'll make you happy, not just successful."

Mel hesitated.

"I'm not asking you to change your life forever, sweetness. Just tonight, just this once, choose something you want to do, not something you feel you have to do."

God, he was doing a number on her. Tearing apart her defenses one by one. "I-I want you," she confessed quietly.

A long thin stream of air whistled from his mouth, like a sigh of relief. "So, what are you going to do about it?"

That sigh of relief, along with the knowledge that he'd hoped this would be her answer, filled her with hope. It filled her with courage too, and with an insatiable need to get him naked. "What am I going to do, or what would I like to do?"

"Let's start with what you'd *like* to do."

She nodded. "Okay. What I'd really like to do is get the hell out of here, go somewhere we can be alone and fuck you until neither of us can stand."

Ben smiled then. A wicked, sexy smile. "Funny you should say that, because it's exactly what I'd like to do too."

For a full second she couldn't breathe. His eyes were so dark with desire she felt she might drown in them.

"Okay, now question number two. What are you *going* to do, sweetness?"

Melissa snorted softly, threw her arms in the air in defeat, and against all odds, smiled. "For once in my life, Benny Boy, I'm going to do exactly what I want to do. If you'll have me for the night, I'm going to go home with you and fuck you until neither one of us can stand."

Ben paid their bill faster than he'd ever paid a bill in his life, tugged her out of the restaurant—with perhaps a tad too much enthusiasm, if her surprised laughter was anything to go by—and hailed the first taxi that came their way. The minute he'd given the driver his address, he pounced, pulling her into his arms and kissing her. Kissing her the way he'd wanted to kiss her since she'd walked into his office that morning.

Kissing her with every ounce of lust and love and respect that had built over the last two weeks.

He didn't stop kissing her until the taxi pulled up outside his unit in Balmain, and even then he had difficulty pulling away. Mostly because Melissa would not release his lips.

And when he finally, finally had her in his flat and the door was closed behind them, he led her into his bedroom, stripped her of her clothes and let her fuck him until neither of them could stand.

Then and only then, did Ben do the other thing he wanted to do. He pulled her close, wrapped his arms around her and fell asleep with the woman he loved by his side.

Chapter Ten

"Damn, Mel. You're sitting in front of me, not lying in your bed on the other side of the city."

"I know, but still, I've grown kind of used to waking up this way. I like it. Don't want to miss out on it this morning."

He shook his head in amusement. "So rather than making love to you, I have to jerk off while you watch?"

"Mm hm." She nodded. "Pretty much."

Her sleepy, hazel gaze was fixed on his dick, making it grow in his hand as he stroked himself. "This isn't how it usually works." Not that he minded.

She scrunched up her nose. "You don't usually masturbate like this?"

"This is precisely how I masturbate. I mean that usually when we're on the phone, you're playing with yourself too."

She smiled. That same smile that lit up his office. The very one he'd have done anything to see a few weeks ago now lit up his bedroom. "So what? You want me to touch myself while you stroke your cock?"

"Yeah, sweetness. That's exactly what I want you to do."

"Well, why didn't you just say so?" She uncurled her long legs from the cross-legged position she'd been sitting in and stretched them in front of her, placing a foot on either side of Ben's legs and bending her knees.

"Oh, yeah," he breathed, as her new position exposed her most private of parts to him.

"That better?" she asked.

He admired her pussy, her lips pink and swollen from their night of lovemaking. "Way better. Way, way better." Moisture beaded on those lips, glistening in the early morning light. "Now...touch yourself."

She did, slipping a finger right over those damp folds and playing to her heart's content.

Ben watched, intrigued. He couldn't look away. "That is...so...fucking hot."

"You like?" Her question was innocent, asked as though she had no idea the effect she was having on him, as though she wasn't watching his hand powering over his cock, up and down, fast as lightning.

"'S'okay," he lied.

"How about this?" She dipped the finger into her pussy.

"'S'also okay, I s'pose." A sheen of sweat formed over his shoulders. That was about the sexiest thing he'd ever seen.

She played with herself languorously, making his mouth as dry as a desert. "Know what I like?"

"Uh-uh." Talking was difficult. "Tell me."

"I like the way you have come leaking out your cock. Like you can't hold it back, can't control it."

"That's 'cause I *can't* hold it back. Seem to...have very little control when...you're around."

"Bet it tastes good." By the sounds of things she'd licked her lips, but Ben had no way of confirming that. She'd moved her finger from her pussy to her clit and was rubbing sensuous circles around the small, swollen bud. No way was he looking anywhere else now.

"I bet you taste better." Christ, she looked delicious.

She drew her finger away from her pussy, and Ben couldn't

137

help but follow its path as she brought it to her face, dipped it into her mouth and sucked on it. Then she smacked her lips together, as though confirming the taste. "It's okay," she told him. "Not as salty as you. Or as musky."

Ben couldn't speak. He just let out a low, long groan instead.

Mel returned her hand to her pussy, played with her clit, slid her finger in her gleaming cunt.

"Ya know, I used to think a hard dick was the sexiest thing about a man." Melissa's voice was a touch lower than usual now. "But now, I'm changing my mind. Now I'm thinking the sexiest thing is a man who wants me to do what makes me happy."

"That's funny, because I'm thinking there's nothing sexier than a woman who's happy with herself, who's happy with what she's doing right now."

"I am happy right now, Ben."

"Me too, sweetness."

"Know what would make me even happier?" Her eyes flashed with sparks of the devil.

"Tell me."

"Watching you come."

Ben groaned. "Wanna come. Badly."

"Do it." The teasing quality in her voice was suddenly gone.

His hand wasn't the only one moving like lighting. Her own was powering away as she drove her finger into her cunt over and over again. Her fingers were wet, her pussy swollen and her breath as ragged as his own.

"A-anything to make you happy."

Ben bottomed out. With his gaze pinned between her legs, and her gaze pinned on his cock, he came. Semen squirted from his dick, shooting straight up into the air before landing with a splat on his stomach.

Mel whimpered.

Another strand shot from him.

Her whimper turned to a low moan. She lifted her hips, pushed her finger in deeper and cried out. Then she too was coming, her body convulsing before him, her thighs and hips jerking on the bed.

He pumped himself dry. Pumped until his dick softened in his hand and his stomach was splattered with a sticky white mess. He pumped until Melissa collapsed, her finger slipping from her pussy as tiny tremors still shook through her.

And then, and only then, did he let go and collapse back on the bed.

He had no idea how he was ever going to find the strength to get up and go to work.

They arrived late that morning. First the taxi had to make a detour past Melissa's place so she could get clean clothes, and then, since neither of them had found time to eat before leaving Ben's place, he insisted on stopping at the coffee shop just outside the lobby of their office, sitting at a table and grabbing a bite. Mel ordered yogurt, he a slice of banana bread. Both had large coffees.

Melissa felt indulged. She hadn't run this morning, a routine she almost never missed, and somehow the skipped exercise felt almost as decadent as their night of passion.

She also felt happy and carefree, a sensation she hadn't experienced in forever. She liked it. Heaps.

But beneath all the happiness and cheer was a strange

unease. Ben wanted her to be happy always. Not just now. She wanted it too. Having experienced it for the last few weeks, she wasn't ready to give it up. Unfortunately, she had no idea how to turn her current state of cheerfulness into a permanent way of being.

Because the bottom line was, she couldn't be happy if she continued working at Preston Elks. And she couldn't leave Preston Elks. She still had to make partner. Still had to prove to herself—the high school failure—that she could do it.

And therein lay another problem. How could she make partner if she was too busy being happy with Ben? She hadn't been able to work *and* play when Thomas was in her life, so how could she possibly do both with Ben?

Ben had not repeated his words of love again, but she felt it in his every action, his every look. Yes, it still freaked her the hell out. Just like their conversation in the restaurant had. He'd seen straight through her, straight past all her defenses, and into her soul. He knew she hated work, knew why she drove herself like she did.

She knew she should run. Sprint as fast and as far away from him as she could go. But as she'd realized last night, he wouldn't let her and she didn't want to. It would be the prudent thing to do, but damn it, hanging out with Ben was too much fun, too...special to give up.

She was developing feelings for him she had no business developing. Beginning to like him altogether too much. What she felt for Ben went way past the simple crush that had motivated her to strip in his office that night.

What if spending a few extra hours with him a week didn't interfere with her plans to make partner? It wasn't like she was about to up and quit her job just to be with him. She still had her long-term goals in place. Nothing had changed. Just because Ben had questioned them didn't mean she was questioning them, or that she was any less determined.

Problem was, his questions had got her thinking. Was there something she wanted to do more than investment banking? Was she happy to stay where she was?

For the next little while she'd decided to continue with things just the way they were. Working to make partner and sleeping with Ben as often as she could. If at any point her work started to suffer, they'd have to cut all personal ties. It would be hard, almost impossible, but she'd done it with Thomas, she could do it with Ben. And when the inevitable hurt and pain came, well, she'd just deal with it then.

As she took a sip of her cappuccino, someone called out behind them.

"Yo, Benny Boy."

Melissa froze. No, she'd never heard the voice before, but she had no doubt who was there.

Ben stood, confirming her fears with his greeting.

"Will." He stuck out his hand, and Melissa watched as he clutched the other man's palm in his and gave a friendly shake.

Her heart thundered. Her breath vanished.

Dear Lord. It was one thing fucking Ben in his office while another man watched. Windows kept them apart. Buildings.

It was another thing altogether when that voyeur stood inches away—in person.

For a good few seconds she sat, immobile, terrified. And then Ben's hand was on her shoulder, warm, supportive, urging her up.

She pasted her most professional, aloof expression on her face and stood to greet the man who'd watched as Ben had, at various times, placed his hand, his tongue and his dick in her pussy. And her arse.

"Melissa, meet Will Granger. Will, Melissa Sparks."

She took the hand he offered, and he shook hers with a firm grip, his palm cool, his fingers long. A tiny shiver raced up Melissa's spine.

"Nice to meet you."

"You too."

"Morning tea?" He released her hand and motioned to the coffee.

"Yeah." And breakfast, but Will didn't need to know that. "You too?"

"Uh-huh. Got a break between clients. Thought I'd grab a coffee."

"Will's a lawyer," Ben explained.

"Ah, any specific area?"

"Family law. With a special interest in adoption. Intercountry adoption."

"Wow, really?" Melissa was instantly more curious about him. "My sister and brother-in-law looked into adoption a few years back. They consulted a lawyer about finding a child outside of Australia. But the whole procedure would have been so long and complicated they didn't go through with it." It had been a difficult, heart-wrenching decision for her sister and brother-in-law.

"I empathize. The process is lengthy and frustrating."

"It must be insanely hard for you too, and you go through it often."

"It is. But when an adoption goes through, and the couple finally gets to bring home their child, it's all worth it."

Melissa smiled, liking Will yet still feeling an undercurrent of unease. Not from him, mind you. It was all her.

Here he stood, in front of her, talking to her. Not separated by thick panes of glass. Sure, she already had a vague impression of what he looked like. She'd have recognized him even if he hadn't been with Ben, but the impact of seeing him in person made her nervous as hell.

Ben had described him as not bad looking. The portrayal didn't do him justice.

The man was gorgeous. Tall, even taller than Ben, and blond with penetrating blue eyes. His lips were full, lush, the kind of lips that invited kisses from complete strangers. High cheekbones and a square jaw, surrounded by tanned skin and an expensive-looking suit and trendy tie, completed the picture of absolute professionalism.

And when he smiled, exposing a cute dimple in his left cheek, her breath left her body.

She let the conversation run dry, very conscious of who he was and what he'd seen.

Will must have felt it too, but unlike her, he didn't hide behind his awkwardness. "Ben has impeccable taste," he said. "Seeing you through my window, I thought you were lovely. From up close? You're perfect."

Flustered by his directness, Melissa wasn't sure how to respond. What was one supposed to say when a man acknowledged he'd observed your sexual encounters with another man?

More than that, Melissa wasn't sure what to make of her physical reaction to him. Her cheeks grew warm under the directness of his gaze, her breasts tightened and her belly fluttered. Arousal or embarrassment?

Ben saved her the trouble of a responding, distracting Will with a question. "So, soccer on Saturday? Are we on?"

143

"Yeah, mate. We are. But they changed the schedule. Instead of playing at four, the game's at three. That work for you?"

"Sure. Either time is good."

Ben played soccer? She'd had no idea. But it didn't surprise her. His strong, athletic build suited that of a soccer player.

"Cool. Come early, about two thirty. The team can get in a practice for half an hour first."

Ben nodded. "No worries."

"'Kay." Will pointed to the counter. "My coffee is ready. I gotta get going." He turned to Melissa. "It was nice to meet you...finally."

"Nice to meet you too."

He smiled. A broad, sexy smile. The man was gorgeous, no two ways about it.

Not quite as gorgeous as Ben—no one was quite as gorgeous as Ben—but he was up there.

"Later." And with that, he collected his take-away and strode off, the confidence in his steps incredibly appealing.

Melissa watched him go. Watched him, with her heart pounding and her hands trembling, until he'd walked through the door and disappeared outside.

"He's gone now," Ben said gruffly. "You can stop staring."

"Stop staring? Sheesh, Ben. That's *him*. That's...Will." *Duh.* As if she needed to tell Ben who he was.

"Yep, that's him." He sat, leaving her with little option but to do the same.

She swallowed, the vein in her neck beating so hard she could feel it. Couldn't Ben see how uncomfortable the whole meeting had made her? Coming face to face with a man who'd seen her naked, who'd seen her in multiple sexual positions, was possibly the single most excruciating moment of Melissa's life. It might also be one of the most exciting. "He's...the *one*."

"Yeah, he is."

"I didn't expect to run into him. Not at all. It never entered my head that I might actually meet him one day."

Ben looked at her carefully. "He works next door. You didn't think running into him would be a distinct possibility?"

She shook her head. "Stupid of me, I know. But there you have it." She wiped her sweaty palms on her skirt. The meeting had her skittish and out of sorts.

"You're surprised?"

"Uh, yeah."

"Shocked?"

"A...a bit."

He narrowed his eyes, then leaned in close and asked softly, so only she could hear, "Excited?"

A jolt went through her. "I—" Heat flooded between her legs. She tried to form a sentence, to say something logical, but in the end could express nothing but the absolute truth. "Yes."

Ben leaned in closer, spoke even more softly. "How excited?"

"V-very."

"Excited by the prospect of him watching us, or by meeting him?"

She couldn't separate them out. "Both."

"Do you find him attractive?" Ben's voice was hoarse.

"He's good looking."

"He turns you on?"

Melissa faltered. She was turned on. No two ways about it.

But was it Will that had her all worked up, or was it the fact that meeting him had automatically made her think of fucking Ben? Because that was the context in which she associated Will. A voyeur to her and Ben's sexual activities. "Meeting him turned me on."

"Tell me, Mel..." His voice was so low she had to pay him her full attention to catch every word. "How would you feel if I took you upstairs now, locked my office door and fucked you in front of my open window—knowing the man you've just met was watching us?"

Oh, God. The very thought of Ben making love to her made Melissa whimper. The idea of Will watching made her pussy clench. Desire for Ben hit her with such force, her hands shook. Had she been holding her coffee, it would have spilled everywhere.

"You'd like that, sweetness, wouldn't you?"

She nodded, helpless to do anything else.

"Would you let him see everything? Would you want him to see everything?"

"I..." She lowered her voice to match his. "Yes. Absolutely everything."

"You'd want him to see you naked?"

She closed her eyes, imagined Ben making love to her while Will watched, seeing everything. The image made her shiver, and she nodded.

"You want him to see me finger you?"

Almost as much as she wanted to be fingered by Ben. Another shiver, another nod.

"How about licking you? Would you like him to watch as I feast on your sweet pussy?"

The idea of Ben's mouth on her cunt was almost more than

she could bear. "S-so much."

"And if I fucked you while he watched, would I take your pussy or your arse?"

"D-do I have to choose?" Could he be that cruel? That withholding? She wanted Ben in every way possible.

"You'd want both?"

"Yes."

"In front of him?"

She nodded.

"What if..." Ben's voice trailed off.

"What if what?"

"Nothing."

"Ben, please. What if what?"

He looked at her with eyes black as night. His mouth was set in a grim line.

"Ben?"

"What if Will wasn't in his office when I fucked you? What if he was in mine?"

Chapter Eleven

Damn it, he'd done it again. Thrown her completely off her game. Had her attention focused elsewhere, so work just wasn't important.

What if Will *was* in Ben's office the next time they made love? How *would* she feel?

She hadn't answered Ben, hadn't been able to. She still didn't have an answer. The idea sent shivers of anticipation racing up and down her spine. It made her breath shallow and her stomach all fluttery.

Melissa blinked in surprise. When had she started using the terms *fucking Ben* and *making love to him* interchangeably? More importantly, when had she begun to think of being with Ben sexually as making love? What had happened to the simple, no-strings-attached affair?

Melissa needn't worry about strings anymore. She'd gone way past that. At some point over the last few weeks she'd brought in the heavy artillery, attaching herself to him with ropes, chains, shackles and irons.

Listless, she stared at the paperwork on her desk. A new company was looking to make investments. One she'd never worked with before but had heard noise about in the field.

Melissa wanted to get excited about the prospect. Wanted the shivers up her spine to be an indication that her work turned her on. They weren't.

She'd met with the CFO a few days ago and gotten a good feel about him. Now she had to back up that feeling with facts and figures of company performance, solid proof they could indeed put up the millions they were looking to offer as debt.

She forced herself to work. Forced herself to do the necessary research, check through Alistair's documents meticulously, and she despised every minute of it. There had been a time when coming to work excited her. When the thrill of knowing she'd gotten such a brilliant job had been enough to spur her on, get her out of bed in the morning, make her rub her hands together at the thought of all she could achieve.

But that time had passed long ago. All that was left now was the drive to do better. Although maybe "obsessive need" would be a more appropriate description than drive.

She let her mind wander. Allowed herself to play *what-if*. What if she left the job? Resigned and did something else altogether? What if she could work in any field, any industry of her choice? What would it be?

She had no idea.

She narrowed down her options. What could she do with her various degrees that would make her happy? Remaining in the business world but moving into a different area of finance did not appeal at all. Yep, there were many high-powered jobs out there that she was qualified to perform in and would offer her stable income and a chance for growth, but she wasn't interested in any of them.

The problem was that she wasn't passionate about business.

Okay, she had a mind for figures. She understood numbers. Could she do something with that? Teach, maybe? Lecture at a university or TAFE? Did she want to do that?

She had no idea. She'd never thought about it before. But teaching someone a new fact, helping them understand something that had previously made no sense did hold a certain amount of appeal.

Maybe something to file away and consider in the future.

Or maybe she could write? She had zero imagination, so fiction would be out. But what about nonfiction? An idiot's-guide-to-investment-banking type of book?

Pfft. She had no idea if there was even a need for another guide to capital investment.

Okay, what about something totally unrelated to numbers or to her current job. What if she became an aroma therapist? Or a reflexologist? Or took up practicing Reiki?

She laughed out loud at that one. Once she'd gone for an aromatherapy massage and had hated every minute of it. While she enjoyed being touched by someone she desired—Ben—she hated being touched all over by someone she didn't know. Hated the invasion of privacy.

She knew she'd hate invading someone else's privacy in the same way.

She could always go back to uni, study something different. But the very idea made her shudder. She'd studied for over nine years. Enough was enough.

Nope. See? Considering alternative job options was a pointless exercise. She was working in a job she was well qualified to do, had gained brilliant experience in, was good at, and most importantly, it held doors open to her. Doors to further success. No point looking at anything else. She was in investment banking for the long haul.

And with that thought, she pushed further deliberation from her mind, refused to think about Ben—or Will, for that matter—any longer, and got down to serious work.

Night came before she left the office. And when she did, it was to nip home to pack an overnight bag and head back to

Ben's place.

She couldn't wait to see him again. Be with him again. Kiss him. Make love to him...

He greeted her with a long, hot kiss and promises of a good meal. He didn't disappoint. Ben served her fresh salad with extra cheese and olives on the side, sumptuous steak grilled to perfection and fresh strawberries for dessert. A crisp Chardonnay was the perfect accompaniment to the meal, although she was the only one sipping it. Ben stuck to scotch.

And when she'd taken her final bite of dinner and pushed her plate aside, he pounced.

They made love on the floor beside his dining room table.

After showering together, they cleared away the dishes and sat down to watch TV.

Melissa marveled at the domesticity of it all, marveled at how comfortable she felt with him, how happy.

"Do you know when last I turned on the telly?" she asked.

"Nope."

"Me neither. I never watch. Never seem to have the time."

"Not even before you go to sleep?"

"I read then. Can't fall asleep without getting through at least a chapter every night."

"And I need to lose myself in some mindless TV program to fall asleep." He grinned mischievously. "Wanna hear a secret?"

"Yeah. Course I do." Especially when he grinned like that. It made her want to hear everything he had to tell her.

"You know what I watch every night?"

"Nope."

"*Home and Away.*"

She gaped at him. "The soapie?"

"Uh-huh."

"You watch a soap opera?"

"Every single night."

She shook her head with a laugh as she digested that piece of information. "But hang on. *Home and Away* isn't on TV late at night." Everyone knew the program was screened early in the evening.

"I know." Another huge grin. "I record it."

"You do not!"

"Do too."

"Do not."

"Do too."

"Fine, then tell me who the main characters are."

"You'd know them?"

She rolled her eyes. "I'd have to be dead not to. I was addicted as a teenager."

"Fine, but don't say you didn't ask." And with that, Ben launched into a detailed description not only of every character on the show—some of whom Melissa had never heard about—but he also told her every sordid detail of every single relationship and every plotline for the last two years, at least.

She stared at him, amazed. "You really do watch."

He grinned triumphantly. "Told you."

"You're crazy."

"I know. And I get really grumpy if I miss an episode."

"But...you missed an episode last night." She'd know, seeing as she'd been with him the entire night. "And tonight."

He nodded. "Yep."

The penny dropped. "Oh. I get it. The reason you're telling me. You want to watch now."

He smiled as he nodded.

"Seriously?"

"Seriously."

Lord, how could she possibly deny him the pleasure? How could she deny him anything? "Well, go ahead, you crazy fool."

And for the next hour, she and Ben watched a soap opera she hadn't watched since she was in school. She enjoyed every minute of it, mostly because she was tucked close against his side, and while adverts were on, instead of fast forwarding through them, Ben took her mouth in long, drugging kisses.

By the time the final credits of the second episode ran, they were both naked again, and Ben was lying on top of her, condom already in place.

"You never did answer my question, sweetness."

"Which one?" Her hands were trailing up his back, relishing the hard muscle beneath the firm skin.

"The one about Will."

Melissa inhaled. Just like that, her body turned to liquid, her internal temperature shooting up.

Ben groaned. "Shit, Mel. Your nipples just got harder."

She reached blindly for his mouth and kissed him. He kissed her straight back, and as she wound her legs around his waist, he slid inside her.

"Wet," he gasped. "So wet." He thrust into her, slowly, repeatedly, as though he couldn't help it, couldn't stop himself. "Wet for me, or...wet for him?"

"For you." For sure. She met Ben thrust for thrust, glorying in the sensations she'd only ever experienced with him.

"Would you want him—" *thrust,* "—there, with us—" *another thrust,* "—in the same room, while—" *thrust,* "—we made love?"

153

Would she? How would she feel if Ben's friend, his ménage partner, stood in the room with them?

Horny as the devil, she suspected.

She nuzzled Ben's neck, nipped his earlobe and whispered softly. "Yes."

A growl escaped from him, a sound unlike any she'd heard before. He drove into her, harder, deeper.

She held him tighter, closer. Dug her nonexistent nails into his back, took him in as far as she could. Still he wasn't close enough. With Ben she just wanted him closer. "But..."

"But...?" His voice was ragged.

"But I wouldn't just want him to watch."

Ben lost his rhythm, jerking against her before finding his tempo again. "W-what else would you...want?"

She closed her eyes, knew her face was scarlet. She also knew she was about to utter the absolute truth again—just like Ben had insisted on last night—and that truth notched her desire up to another level. "For him to join in."

Another of those gruff growls escaped Ben.

Since the moment Ben had told her about his and Will's threesomes, she'd been curious. Interested. Aroused. "I'd want him to fuck me while you and I made love." She was careful to make the distinction. Careful to let Ben know there would be a distinction.

Ben reacted.

"Ah, fuck... Mel!" He went wild. Lost control. Lost the beautiful rhythm of his thrusts. He slammed into her, repeatedly, moving fast and hard, bucking up and roaring.

Melissa cried out, the raw passion of his actions calling out to her own lust, making her just as wild, just as uncontrolled. And the fact that she'd shared her secret desire with him, confessed to something she *wanted* to do, just made her hotter, hungrier.

She shoved her hips up to meet his every reckless plunge, pulled her legs further up his waist, giving him more room, opening herself wider to his carnal attack.

And when he roared, loud and low, and reared up, Melissa came. Her orgasm descended, wiping conscious thought from her mind. The only thing she was aware of, other than the incendiary pleasure that crashed over her, was Ben's own release as he slammed into her one last time before pulsing and shuddering inside her.

Much to Ben's satisfaction, Melissa spent not only Friday night with him, but Saturday and Sunday nights as well. She even went along to watch his soccer match, dressing in his team colors to show her support. When Will and the rest of the team went for drinks afterwards, Melissa was happy to tag along. She wasn't the only woman. Several players had partners with them.

Ben was merciless with her. He sat beside her, with Will and the rest of the team all around them, and between making small talk and laughing with the boys, he whispered filthy things in her ear. Made lewd, wicked suggestions about all the things he and Will could do to her, given the chance.

The more suggestions he made, the redder Mel's face became. She began to breathe raggedly, and her hazel eyes turned dark with desire. Once again, in the middle of a pub, with a crowd of people surrounding him, Ben got an erection. A huge boner. And it didn't go down anytime soon.

Melissa noticed. Her smile was triumphant.

Not one to wilt under the pressure of his teasing, Melissa

took great pleasure in flirting with the other players, making him jealous as hell. His teammates took it good-naturedly, seeing it for what it was—a way of winding Ben up.

Ben took it well too, laughing along with the boys and throwing his arm around Melissa, pulling her closer. Staking his claim in front of all of them. In front of Will.

It satisfied him no end when Mel cuddled into him, molding her curves to his side.

Will watched them both. Ben was aware of the way his gaze lingered on Melissa, was aware of the way Melissa kept sneaking looks at Will.

It turned him the fuck on. Made him want to get naked with Melissa and Will. Made him want to take her right there on the floor while Will took her from the other side.

It also made him want to slam his fist in Will's face. Made him want to hurt the man who'd become his closest mate. Made him want to get Melissa the hell away from him, as fast as he could. And when Melissa intimated to Ben that she might just mosey on over to Will and chat with him about the hypothetical dynamics of a threesome, Ben cut her off with a hard, hungry kiss.

Yeah, he knew she'd been joking, ragging on him, but the thought of her actually doing it sent him into a jealous rage. As arousing as the thought of sharing Melissa with Will was, it also chafed. Big-time.

Minutes later, Ben pretty much hauled her out of the pub in his eagerness to get her naked and alone. Melissa went along happily. They left to the sound of loud cheers from his teammates. He took her home and made love to her in the privacy of his own bed.

But Ben knew he was in deep trouble. He'd been the one to put the idea of a threesome in Melissa's mind, but she was the one getting excited at the mere thought of it.

Melissa masked her face with an expressionless look as she read the text message on her iPhone.

Boardroom.

10 p.m.

No clothes required.

She deleted it. It was after all, a work phone, and God knew who else might have access to it. Then, with her face as blank as she could keep it and her knees trembling beneath the table, she smiled at the CFO of Hymand & Clark and spent the next two hours briefing him about a company he'd shown interest in investing in.

Halfway through the meeting, her phone beeped again.

Correction.

Garters required.

And thigh-highs.

Nothing else.

And half an hour after that, Melissa apologized again as she checked her phone once more, explaining with a deadpan face there was a crisis at home. The CFO had no problem with her reading the message while he waited.

Boardroom now?

Not sure I can wait 'til 10.

Thankfully the next message came after the CFO had left.

Boardroom was full.

Lucky you didn't meet me there.

Could have been awkward.

'Specially if you'd worn your garters and nothing else.

Melissa chuckled. Ben knew full well she'd been the one utilizing the boardroom. He also knew full well that his messages would have made concentrating on a work meeting while in that boardroom very difficult.

A short while later, he took her mind off the boardroom.

Boardroom rendezvous too risky.

My house, 10 p.m.

Garters required.

Nothing else.

Melissa rang his bell at 9:59 p.m.

Chapter Twelve

Ben gave her a very thorough once-over, taking in her tailored, knee-length lightweight coat. He raised an eyebrow as he stepped back, letting her inside. "I thought I told you nothing but garters required."

"And I'm pretty sure driving across the city in nothing but garters is a criminal offense." Her hands were on the belt around her waist, unbuckling it.

He grinned and pushed the door closed. "If so, I'd have liked to be the cop dispatched to pull you over."

"You could always pull me over now." She slipped off the jacket, almost bringing Ben to his knees in the process.

Melissa stood before him in nothing but her garters, thigh-highs and heels.

He closed his eyes and offered a quiet prayer of thanks.

It was Will who filled the awed silence. "Perfect," he said. "Absolutely perfect."

Melissa swiveled around, gawking at the man. "Will?"

Will nodded. "Yeah, beautiful. It's me."

Melissa's response was immediate. She stepped back, using Ben to shield her nude form from Will's appreciative gaze.

"You invited him here?" Her eyes were enormous as she stared at Ben.

"I did. For you." Because she wanted him. She'd said as much too many times for him to ignore it. And Ben had resolved to give Melissa whatever she wanted. To show her that pleasure and happiness came from going after what you wanted, not from doing what you thought was the right thing to do.

Tonight Ben knew what he thought was right—and he shoved it aside in favor of doing what Melissa wanted.

She raised a brow. "For me?"

"For your pleasure."

"Ben!" She sounded appalled. Her eyes flashed and her cheeks flushed scarlet. But she didn't reach for her jacket. Didn't try to put it on. Not once.

"He can leave," Ben assured her. "Right now. He'll walk away—if that's what you really want."

"I will." Will's voice was gentle, and Melissa looked at him over Ben's shoulder. "I'll go if you don't want me here."

"Or..." Ben waited until Melissa had returned her gaze to him. "He can stay."

"And do what?" she asked in a husky voice.

"Whatever you want him to do."

"I could do nothing at all," Will offered. "I could just sit here while you and Ben do whatever you two want to."

Melissa's mouth formed into a big, luscious O.

"Or, sweetness, he could do whatever we're doing. He could do it with us." Goosebumps broke out over her skin, and her nipples beaded. Her breasts looked so damn delicious, Ben wanted nothing more than to take them in his mouth and suckle them.

"A-and what will we be doing?"

"Anything you want to do. Anything at all. We could play chess, if you like."

Her lips twitched. "Chess?"

"Monopoly?" Ben offered.

She shook her head. "Board games aren't my thing."

"We could watch telly," Will suggested.

"Home and Away?" Mel's lips twitched, and Ben desperately wanted to kiss them.

"Uh, if that's what you want."

Ben laughed at the surprise in Will's voice. Melissa may know about his weakness for the soapie. Will had not a clue. It wasn't the kind of information a bloke shared with his mates.

"It's not what I want," Melissa said softly.

"What is?" Ben whispered.

"You. Always you." She bit her lip, ran her tongue over it, left it looking moist and inviting. "And just for tonight, Will too."

"Together?"

She looked over at Will again and nodded. "Together."

Conflict assailed Ben instantly. His dick, already firm and erect, swelled further, taking his desire to a whole new level. At the same time his gut clenched as jealousy tore a vicious hole through it.

Melissa wanted Will. Wanted to fuck his friend.

The woman he loved desired another man.

Just like Sienna had.

Sienna had slept with Ben and another man—and she'd chosen the other man.

Would Melissa do the same? When her passion was spent, would she choose Will over him?

Ben forced his fear and jealousy aside. Tonight was not about him. Tonight was about giving Melissa the pleasure and the happiness she'd denied herself for so long. Since the first day Ben had told her about Will, he'd suspected things would reach this point. Every time they made love in front of Will, every time his name was mentioned, Melissa's arousal increased.

Will turned her on.

She wanted Will.

And Ben could not refuse her this experience.

Besides, now that they'd reached this point, the idea of taking her while Will fucked her himself had him sweating. He was kidding himself if he believed this wasn't what he wanted too.

He wanted it. Badly enough to set the whole thing up.

"Then it'll happen," Will promised. "You, me and Ben, together. Soon."

Melissa's eyes widened. "Soon?"

"Not yet."

She shook her head, confused. "So I'm standing here, undressed, my body bared to your gaze and Ben's, and you're telling me not yet?"

"It's a compliment," Will explained. "Seeing you like this is half the pleasure. If it's okay with you, I'd like to stretch that pleasure out."

Ben cupped her cheek, felt the heat of her skin burn his hand. "He likes to watch, sweetness. You should know that by now."

Understanding lit up her eyes. "Of course he does."

"Would that be okay with you, Melissa?"

She smiled, even as her breath hitched. "That would be...perfectly okay with me." And with that, she drew Ben's hand from her cheek and placed it on the mound of her pussy.

Ben didn't hesitate. Couldn't. He slid his hand lower, over the swollen nub of her clit and let his finger delve between her feminine folds.

Well, hell!

The woman was wet, her pussy slick and warm.

"Kiss me, Ben," she whispered. "Make love to me."

A fierce moan escaped him before he was aware it had formed in his throat, and then she was in his arms, and he was kissing her again. Running his tongue over hers, tasting the hunger on her lips.

As for his finger, Christ, his finger was where it had to be, tunneling inside her slippery channel, dipping deep between her velvety walls.

Ben wrapped his free arm around her shoulders, pulling her as close as he could in this position, then he spun them both around, giving Will what he wanted. A clear view of Melissa from behind.

The man had sat back down on the couch opposite them, and just imagining what Will saw inflamed Ben—Melissa's long, toned legs, ending at her firm, slim arse. Her firm, slim, *naked* arse. And the gentle swell of her bare hips and tiny waist. Never mind the wild mane of russet hair that covered her back.

Perfect as the image would be, Ben knew it wasn't enough.

Will would want to see *everything.*

Ben showed him, inserting his knee between Melissa's thighs, forcing her legs wider apart.

Will's soft groan told Ben he'd achieved what he'd intended. From his angle, Will would be able to see Ben's finger moving in and out of Melissa. He added another digit, and Melissa trembled in his arms.

Throughout it all, Ben kissed her. Claimed her mouth for himself.

Melissa twisted, ground herself down on his fingers and

tore at the buttons on his shirt. One or two popped off, and she grabbed his top with both hands and ripped it open all the way. Even as she shoved it over his shoulders, she ground her breasts into his naked chest, pressing her nipples into his skin.

God, would he ever get enough of this woman? Ever tire of sipping from her lips, caressing her breasts, filling her pussy?

He doubted it.

He tore his mouth from hers and dropped his head to her breasts, tugging a distended nipple into his mouth. Her soft cries led him on as he suckled, licked, nipped and kissed her, first one breast and then the other, and though he could have gorged forever, a more urgent need grew within.

"Need to taste you, sweetness. Taste all of you." He dropped to his knees in front of her, buried his head in her groin and within seconds was running his tongue over her clit.

She shook at his ministrations and cried out his name, but still it wasn't enough, still he couldn't taste all of her.

Will also must have thought it wasn't enough. "Show me," he said. "Show me everything."

Ben picked Melissa up, placing an arm beneath her knees and one around her shoulders. He carried her across the room and laid her down on her back on the floor.

"Bend your knees, sweetness," he instructed.

"Like this?" She offered Will an unhindered view between her legs.

"Just like that."

"Perfect," Will growled as he yanked off his shirt.

Ben let him appreciate the sight for maybe three seconds, and then Ben's hunger—and his possessiveness—got the better of him. He crouched above Melissa, a knee on either side of her head, leaned forward and took possession of her gleaming cunt.

In this position there was no obstruction to feasting to his heart's content.

And feast he did, licking Melissa, from her slit to her clit, repeatedly, until she squirmed beneath him, twisting her hips, giving him even better access. As she moaned his name and her body began to tighten in prelude to her orgasm—which Ben anticipated with fervor—she did something he hadn't expected.

Rather than succumb to the passion that had her entire body trembling, she lifted her face and buried her nose in his groin.

"Me too," she whispered. "I need to taste you while you taste me." Her hands were on his zip, and she was opening his pants, pushing them over his hips. Ben kicked off his shoes. Christ, he wanted to focus on her pleasure, wanted to give her a little portion of paradise—an orgasm so strong it took her breath away.

But Melissa took his freed cock in her hands, stroked it and opened her mouth.

Ben forgot what he was doing. He forgot everything save the sensation of those hot, wet lips wrapping around him, pulling him into her mouth. Deep, deeper. Then releasing him.

No, fuck. Don't let go. Ever!

Her tongue was wicked. And wonderful, licking him all over, lapping at his tip, drawing him into her mouth again. She sucked her cheeks in tight, caressing him with their satiny heat, then she scraped her teeth ever so softly against his hypersensitive skin as she released him.

Ben had two choices. He could give himself over to the decadent pleasure of her mouth and come, or he could man up to the occasion, force back the orgasm building in his scrotum and give Melissa the attention she deserved.

He dipped his head back down and slid his tongue over

165

Melissa's dewy lips, lapping at her juices. He refused to think about her mouth or the way it caressed him. Refused to think how easily he could lose control. Ben slid his tongue as far as it could go into her channel.

"Fuck," Will gasped. "That is so fucking hot."

It was hot. And getting steamier by the minute.

Ben had no choice. He had to extricate himself from Mel's torturous mouth. She released him with a wet slurp but wasn't ready to let him go altogether. As he continued to devour her pussy, she trailed the tip of her tongue up and down the length of his shaft.

It felt...subliminal.

"I'd love to see you come, Mel," Will said. "Love to watch you explode all over Ben's tongue."

Melissa whimpered.

"I'm as turned on as you are," Will told her. "Watching you two together, seeing what you do to each other, Christ, it's making me ache."

Melissa withdrew her tongue from Ben's cock as she moved her head. "Y-you're stroking yourself." Her voice was hoarse, raspy as sin.

"It's because of you. Because of what you and Ben are doing. It's about the sexiest damn thing I've ever seen."

"V-very sexy," Melissa agreed. "So s-sexy I'm gonna come. Soon."

Her body trembled.

"Show me," Will encouraged her.

Melissa grabbed Ben's thighs, gripped them tight. A fresh stream of juice slid from her channel.

Ben lapped it up, lapped at her clit, laved her over and over. He luxuriated in the shivers rippling through her, in the

166

throaty moans she couldn't repress. Every one of her muscles tensed beneath him.

Close. She was close. Ben pressed harder on her clit.

"Let go, Melissa," Will instructed. "Come for Ben."

Melissa exploded. Her body tensed and then shuddered. The lips of her pussy clenched beneath his tongue, and her clit was rigid. Her cries filled the air, and her fingertips dug into Ben's hips.

Ben savored her orgasm, licked her through it. God, he loved it when she came, loved watching her let go of her control, let her passionate, wanton side out to play.

The last of her shudders had barely rolled away when Will spoke again. "She looks...delicious."

His voice came from close, real close, and Ben was forced to lift his head to look at him. He knelt at Melissa's feet.

"She is delicious."

Will looked at Melissa's pussy, his expression hungry. "May I?"

Ben looked at Melissa. "May he?"

She answered with a whimper.

"That's a yes," he translated, and scooted back to let his friend have a taste.

The second Will's tongue touched Melissa, she yelped. "Ben!"

"Right here, sweetness." He stroked her hair.

She reached out, found his free hand and clutched it.

"He's... Will's... Oh, God...he's..."

"I know he is, Mel. I'm right here, watching." His heart hammered, and his dick slapped against his stomach. He didn't want to find this arousing, didn't want to be turned on by his friend going down on the woman he loved, but God help him, he loved watching. "How's it feel, sweetness?"

"So good." Her soft moans filled the air.

"Describe it."

"N-naughty. Feels naughty."

"And?"

She paused, panted heavily. "Thrilling. D-different from you."

Ouch. "I'm not thrilling?"

"You're the most thrilling. But with Will...it's...forbidden, enticing."

"And with me?"

A soft, content sigh whispered from her mouth. "With you it's perfect. Every time."

Ben kissed her. Claimed her mouth and kept it. Will could have her pussy—for now. But her mouth, the lips that had called him perfect, were his. Will could do whatever Melissa asked him to do tonight. But he couldn't have her mouth. He couldn't kiss her.

Because that was Ben's job.

Melissa groaned, and Ben captured the sound with his lips, kissing her harder. Within seconds she was twisting, arching her back, whimpering. And then she was coming, climaxing on Will's tongue.

Ben kissed her through it and was gratified to note that not once, no matter how hard she came, did she release his lips. She wanted his kiss as much as he wanted hers.

Chapter Thirteen

Melissa lay supported in Ben's arms, breathless. He'd shifted so he sat behind her and pulled her into the V of his legs, her back to his chest.

The rigid length of his erection pressed against her lower back, and his arms were wrapped around her front. He lent her strength and structure where her body had none, and she leaned into him, gratefully accepting his support, luxuriating in his warmth, his hardness.

Two orgasms, from two incredibly sexy men, in such quick succession, left her winded. And shivery. And sated. Well, half-sated anyway.

Because as exquisite as their joint attack had been so far, it wasn't enough. It wasn't all she wanted. Just for tonight she wanted everything Ben and Will had to give her physically. She wanted both of them, at the same time. And she wasn't thinking about their tongues.

This was an opportunity unlike any she'd ever experienced before, a chance to lose herself to the untold pleasures offered by two talented men.

Ben had challenged her about her lack of a social life, had made her aware of everything she'd given up in order to make herself into a successful woman and banish her fears of future failure.

He'd challenged her, and then he'd done the unbelievable. Given her the social, private and personal life she hadn't allowed herself for years. Not since she'd broken up with

Thomas.

She'd grabbed onto his special gift, clutched it close and made the most of it. She'd let Ben into her heart, started feeling things for him she had no business feeling for anyone.

And now the man who had challenged her to do what she wanted to do, to set goals that would make her happy, had once again paved the way for her to access pleasure and happiness. He'd offered her a threesome. Brought his friend in to play with them for a night.

It blew her mind.

Imagining herself with Ben *and* Will was one thing. Carrying through on those fantasies? Another thing altogether. Alone she'd never have acted. Never have expressed her desire to fuck two men. But she hadn't been alone. Ben was with her, every step of the way. Holding her hand, guiding her through the process.

Just like he'd been holding her hand and guiding her since that first night in his office.

"You doing okay, sweetness?" he asked now.

The caring in his voice reached her heart, settling in there. She smiled and shivered, the after-effect of two incredible orgasms. Or maybe she shivered from the startling realization that Ben meant more to her than she'd ever dreamed he might. "I'm doing great—in case you couldn't tell from my physical responses."

"You had enough yet?" This from Will.

Er, hell no! "Have you?"

He grinned and pointed to his erection. "Does it look like I've had enough?"

His cock was hard, throbbing. Melissa couldn't help wondering what it would be like having both men inside her at the same time.

Would it hurt? Probably. Two penises would be a challenge. But she had no doubt the pleasure would eclipse the pain. The very anticipation of what was to come had her body quivering and heat flowing to her cunt.

Two penises inside her. *Two.*

She returned her gaze to Will's face. "It looks like you have a long way to go before you're ready to call it a day."

Will chuckled. "She's observant, this one," he told Ben. "Doesn't miss a trick."

"Not a single trick," Ben agreed.

Melissa moved his hands so they covered her breasts, and pushed into them. Ben needed no further encouragement. He caressed her breasts, stroked them, pinched lightly at her nipples and then a bit harder, until pleasure mixed with pain and Melissa groaned out loud.

Will regarded Ben with a solemn expression. "What about you, mate? You had enough yet?"

Ben held her tighter, cupped both breasts in his palms. "Truth is, I can't seem to get enough of her, ever."

Just like Mel couldn't seem to get enough of Ben. Ever.

Will nodded. "I can see that. Which is why I'm asking again. Have you had enough of this? Of three of us?"

Mel held her breath, aware of the change of energy in the room. The topic of conversation hadn't changed, but something about Ben and Will had. There was a seriousness in the air that hadn't been there before.

As Will studied Ben, waiting for his response, so Melissa studied Will. And she noticed something interesting. Will had absolute respect for Ben. Ben's answer, whatever it might be, would be final. Will would not question it. If Ben said he'd had enough, Will would leave.

Her heart pounded. Would Ben say enough?

God, she hoped not. Not before she'd had a chance to fuck them both.

But why was Ben hesitating? Had he had enough? He'd set this entire encounter up. Why reconsider now? Wasn't this what he wanted? The length of his erection on her back told her it was. His silence, and the stillness of his hands, told her the opposite.

She couldn't bear the quiet. "Ben?"

He buried his nose in her neck, inhaled. "I can't get enough of you, sweetness. When you're not around, I need to be with you. And when you are around I just want more."

Melissa closed her eyes and whimpered, delighted in his words. She felt exactly the same way. "I want more of you too, Ben. Always. But w-what about when Will is also around? Do you still want more?"

Ben answered her question with a question of his own. "Do you?"

She opened her eyes, looked at Will, appreciated his beauty all over again. "I do." Butterflies rose and fluttered in her belly, and her breasts tightened further. "Just for tonight, I want you both."

"Then just for tonight, that's what I want too." Ben's cock jerked against her back as though confirming his words.

"Show me, Benny Boy," Will said. "Show me how much you want her." His eyes gleamed with desire.

Ben snaked a hand down over her belly, and lower, until his finger slid over the wetness between her legs, sending a jolt of pure lust through her. "I'll need a condom for that," he told Will.

Melissa dropped her head back on Ben's shoulder, closed her eyes and let his touch thrill her, excite her all over again. She thrust against his finger and spread her legs wider. She may have just had two stunning orgasms but already her body prepared for another. Slick heat trickled onto Ben's finger, and she arched her back, hoping he'd dip inside her and fill the hollowness that built steadily with his caresses.

Movement in front of her told her Will had stood up, walked away. Seconds later he was back.

"One for you, one for me."

Ben reached up with his free hand, and something crinkled close to her ear. Still he stroked her.

"Show me," Will said again, and once more he moved away.

"You have the energy to move, sweetness?"

Her limbs felt languorous, lazy, but if moving meant more pleasure from Ben, she'd do it. "Mm-hm."

"Okay, then I need you to turn around. Give me a sec to get this on, and then plant your sweet arse on my lap and wrap your legs around my waist."

With muscles as languid and liquid as hot honey, she slowly twisted and turned until she knelt where Ben wanted her—straddling his lap as he sat on the floor. Will sat behind her, back on the couch.

"That's it, sweetness. Now lower yourself down onto me." Ben held her hips, and watched her with eyes as dark as night. His lips were full and swollen from kissing her—all over—and she couldn't wait to press her mouth against his again, taste his tongue, breathe his air. "Guide me inside," he whispered. "Make me a part of you."

Mel didn't need Ben's cock to know he was already inside of her. Sometime over the past few weeks he'd become a part of her. She took his shaft gently in her hand, held it in place and listened to his groans as she slid her pussy down over the length, enveloping him completely. His eyelids looked heavy, as though he had trouble keeping them open, and a breath of air hissed softly from his mouth.

"Damn... Mel..." And then he stopped talking. Didn't seem able for a few seconds.

Lord, he felt good inside. The hollowness receded with every inch she took him in, replaced by a sense of bone-deep satisfaction and crazy-arsed desire. Ben made her crazy. Made her feel wanton and sexy and loved and adored. Ben made her feel. Full stop.

"He's loving this, Mel," Will whispered. "He's in heaven."

Ben wasn't the only one. "I am too," she whispered back.

"I've never seen him look like that before," Will said. "As though he's found his very own piece of paradise inside you." His voice was filled with a soft reverence.

"You are my paradise, sweetness," Ben said softly. His hands crept up her back and tunneled in her hair.

Just like he had become her paradise. She dropped the softest kisses on his lips as warmth filled every inch of her being.

Long moments later, Melissa had to clear her throat to speak. Emotion made forming words difficult. "Will?"

"Yeah?"

"Are you going to join us?"

"Soon," he promised. "Very soon. But watching you two, together, it..." He inhaled deeply. "It takes my breath away. I could watch you all night."

Shivers raced up her spine. "It's pleasurable for you?"

Will nodded and gave her a beautiful smile, his dimple

creasing his cheek. "Intensely pleasurable." His hand was once again wrapped around his shaft, and his blue eyes were now almost as dark as Ben's. "Make it even more so. Make love to Ben while I watch. Kiss your lover."

Melissa was only too happy to comply. She turned her head into Ben's waiting kiss and lost herself to his taste and to Will's gaze.

Ben pulled away to change positions. "Wrap your legs around my waist, sweetness. Take me in as deep as you can."

It was awkward, but with Ben's help she managed, and the change in position seated Ben's cock deeper inside her.

"Now what?" As if she needed direction. Instinct told her what to do, but she liked Ben giving her instructions.

"Now wrap your arms around my neck." His hands were on her back, caressing her up and down the length of it.

She obeyed. "And now?"

Will answered. "Now you kiss him again."

"Gladly." She melded her mouth to Ben's.

And for the longest time, instructions weren't necessary. They moved together as one, Melissa riding Ben, Ben stroking up into her. Their lips and tongues tangled together as Will whispered words of encouragement.

Making love to Ben while Will had watched through his window was a thrill. Making love to Ben, with Will right behind her, had shivers whizzing up and down her spine. It had her pussy wetter than it had ever been, and it had her skin tingling.

Ben kissed her as though his life depended on it. Kissed her as though he treasured and adored her, and she kissed him right back, returning all his enthusiasm.

"Benny Boy?" Will said eons later.

Ben broke the kiss. "Hmmm?"

"Show me her arse."

"You got it." He kissed her again before asking her, "Ready?"

She nodded, not quite sure what she was ready for, but ready nevertheless.

Ben stretched his legs out beneath her, held her carefully and began to lean back. Melissa had no choice. She had to climb onto her knees again or risk having her legs squashed beneath Ben. She crouched over him, but only until he was on his back, and then he was urging her down again, urging her closer. She knelt with her knees on either side of his waist and lowered her upper body down to meet his.

Ben took her mouth in a bone-melting kiss while he stroked into her. He placed a hand on each of her butt cheeks and pulled them slightly apart, seating himself deeper inside her.

She lost herself to the wonder of his lovemaking, to the shivers down her spine, to the knowledge that Will could see not only her arse, but every thrust of Ben's shaft inside her.

And when something cool and slippery touched her crack, Melissa yelped.

She should have known to expect it, should have realized it was coming. But she'd been so absorbed in Ben's lovemaking, in his kisses, in him, the touch came as a surprise.

She relaxed into it, let Will's finger caress her hole as Ben fucked her. Let Will rub erotic circles around her anus, let him up the ante, increasing her arousal about ten times over.

And when Will dipped his finger inside her, past the ring of muscle keeping him out, Melissa groaned out loud.

"That's it, beautiful," he encouraged. "Just settle in and enjoy yourself."

Settle in? Was he nuts? How could anyone this turned on settle in?

He slipped another finger inside her, slid them both deep.

She gasped. It was a tight fit, but damn, it felt good.

"I feel it too, sweetness." Ben never lost his tempo, although perspiration beaded on his forehead. "I feel the pressure."

"More," Melissa demanded.

A third finger breached her arse.

She gasped. Okay. Even tighter. Fuller. But it just made Ben feel that much better inside her.

Will pumped his fingers in and out, timing his rhythm to Ben's movements. And when Melissa began to whimper, because she couldn't seem to help herself, he withdrew them.

"Nooo!" No, no, no. That was the last thing she wanted.

"Shh, Mel. I'm not going anywhere. Promise."

Quite the opposite, he stepped in close. Or maybe knelt in close, the hair from his muscled leg pressing against the back of her thigh.

She had no idea how he was positioned, couldn't turn to see. Ben had captured her gaze with his, and she couldn't look away. He stared so deep into her eyes she thought he might be seeing through to every thought in her head, every feeling in her heart.

Could he understand them? Could he make sense of the montage of emotions swirling around inside, sort through the tangle of thoughts in her mind? Could he see she'd fallen for him, hard? She stared back at Ben, looked into his dark eyes and lost herself in them.

She sighed. What a perfect place to get lost. She almost wished she'd never find her way back.

Will brought her back. Or the pressure on her arse did.

This time it wasn't his fingers that stroked at her hole. It was just as cool, just as slippery as his hand had been, but it was bigger, thicker.

Melissa didn't dare breathe. She lay where she was, aware that even Ben had stilled as she opened herself for Will's invading cock.

"I'm wearing a condom," Will assured her. "And a ton of lube. Gonna make this good for you, beautiful. Gonna make this good for all three of us."

"Trust him," Ben said. "Let him in."

How could she not? Already he'd breached her hole, leaving her with no doubt of the thickness of his cock. She'd never had anything that large inside her backside before.

Now Ben wasn't the only one sweating. Perspiration slithered down Melissa's spine.

Could she do this? Could she fit them both in? Perhaps the reality wasn't quite as exciting as the fantasy, after all.

Ben stilled, aware of her discomfort. "It'll only last a minute," he promised. "Then the pleasure will mask the pain."

"B-burns a bit."

Will hesitated, then withdrew slowly from her.

She hated that he'd left her. Swore at him. "No, fuck. What are you doing?"

"Just giving you time to adjust, that's all." And then he was sliding back inside her, deeper this time. And the burn was still there, but not quite as bad as before.

"Deeper," she demanded.

He pushed in further.

Ben groaned.

"And again." She wanted him in all the way. Wanted them

both inside her.

Will withdrew once more, but before she had time to complain he drove slowly back inside.

Ben shut his eyes and moaned, and Melissa relaxed fully into Will's thrust.

It was Will's turn to moan. "I'm in. All the way. And damn, it feels good."

Melissa couldn't breathe. Couldn't think. Full. She was so full. Jam-packed full of cock. One in each hole. It burned, but when Ben moved, seating himself deeper inside her, a shock of pleasure pulsed through her.

It was so damn amazing, she twisted her hips, seeking an instant replay.

Will howled, pulled out and thrust back inside her. He grabbed her hips, holding her firmly, and Melissa could have cried the sensations were so exquisite. Her instinct had been right. The pain didn't go away, but the pleasure masked it.

She was sandwiched between two males, both in the prime of their lives. Solid muscled cushioned her front, and raw power emanated from behind her.

How could one woman stand so much masculinity?

How could she not?

"Fuck me," she begged, her physical appetite for the men insatiable. "Please, both of you, just fuck me." Her greedy words echoed through the room. She knew then this wasn't about making love. Making love was what she and Ben did when they were alone. This was sex in the rawest, most physical sense of the word.

"It'll be our pleasure," Will said.

"Just lie down and enjoy the ride, sweetness." And as Ben took her mouth in yet another kiss, he and Will began to fuck her in earnest. It wasn't hard to tell they'd done this before. Many times. They moved in perfect harmony, one filling her while the other withdrew. Every now and again they moved together, filling her at the same time, and that for Melissa was the ultimate.

She'd never felt this good, this aroused. Never known that two men could increase her pleasure and her excitement exponentially. They incited her passions, made her body burn. Goose bumps covered her skin, and her breath was a thin rasp of delight.

"I-is it as good for you...as for me?" she wanted to know.

"Better," was Will's response. Ben nodded vigorously.

"Can...can you feel each other?" She could feel them both so clearly, and she wondered, separated as they were by a thin membrane, if they could feel it too.

"Hard not to, sweetness. Every time he fucks you, I feel it along the length of my dick," Ben said. "Like an increased pressure, a sensual stroke."

Melissa groaned, the image so sensory she could almost feel it herself.

"And every time Ben fucks you, his scrotum touches mine."

Oh, sweet heaven. Boy bits touching. Wow. That was a turn-on she'd never expected. It brought a fresh wave of heat to her loins. "D-do you like it?"

Ben tunneled his fingers into her hair. "I'm so aroused right now, any touch is titillating. Yours and Will's. But his bits don't turn me on. You do." And then there was no more talking. Just fucking. And kissing.

And pleasure. Raw, animalistic, wanton pleasure. And pain. More pleasure though. Way more. Enough to inspire another orgasm. It built inside Melissa, rose higher and higher with each carnal thrust. She thought she might burst from it. Thought the sheer bliss of having both men inside her might make her explode.

It was Ben who reached his peak first. When he cried out and spasmed inside her, his cock pulsing over and over as Will continued to fuck her, Melissa could hold back her release no longer. The intensity of Ben's climax broke her. She loved it when he orgasmed. It sent her rocketing into another plane, a plane where pleasure and passion and rapture ruled.

She came. Came so damn hard. Her muscles clamped around the two cocks inside her, held them both tight, then, unable to resist the impulse, released them. Again and again she convulsed on those two penises, fully aware of the men she was sandwiched between. The one behind her, so sexy, yet so unknown, and the one beneath her, so dear and so familiar. And just as sexy. No, more so.

Ben and Will were making her come. Ben and Will had inspired a wicked, wanton, dirty orgasm, and Melissa loved every single millisecond of it.

As her cries echoed off the wall, Will shouted behind her. And then he too was coming, his cock throbbing in her arse as he took his release.

Their combined cries and groans bounced off the walls. The scent of sex filled the air. The smell of desire and lust and spent passion. Long moments passed before Melissa's heartbeat returned to normal, before her world stopped spinning, before she was cognizant of where she was.

She'd slumped atop Ben, her breasts squashed against his chest, her belly pressed into his stomach. And Will was strewn atop her back, his chest and stomach resting above her, his arms flopping at her sides.

No one moved for a very long time.

Chapter Fourteen

Hours after Will left, hours after Ben had drawn a long, hot, soothing bath for her and washed away every trace of stickiness, Melissa awoke in Ben's bed. She rolled over, seeking out his heat and strength so she could curl back up and fall asleep again.

But Ben wasn't there.

She was alone, with only the doona to keep her warm.

With nothing to do but wait for him to return, she let her mind wander. Her breath caught as she relived the perfection of the evening. Physically, it had been an adventure, a journey into the forbidden. A journey steeped with pleasure, excitement, thrills and taboos. Already she'd filed it away in a little imaginary folder of incredible experiences.

Emotionally, the experience had been life-altering. It had changed something inside Melissa. Softened a part of her she'd believed had hardened forever—her heart. Weeks ago she'd lost that same heart to Ben and then done everything in her power to pretend she hadn't. Now she'd let him into it.

It was time to stop denying the truth. Time to acknowledge that whatever was happening between the two of them was real. Real enough that Melissa was having massive internal debates. She was rethinking her decision to forego a social life in favor of work and questioning her determination to not become involved—long term—with a man.

After tonight, she knew for sure she wanted Ben for more than a temporary fling. She wanted him for her happiness, her contentment and for her peace of mind. He'd become her reason for waking up in the morning and her reason for looking forward to work. He'd become everything she'd never allowed into her life, and now that he was there, now that he was a part of her, she never wanted to let him go.

Ben's generosity took her breath away. He'd organized the entire evening. Set it up for her. He'd put her pleasure before his own so she would experience everything she'd secretly longed for and never allowed herself.

Sure, he'd had threesomes before—with women he didn't care about. But Ben cared about Melissa. He'd told her as much. Told her he loved her. Wow. What a way to show it.

How could she not want the man in her life on a permanent basis?

Sleep eluded her. After what she'd done tonight with Ben and Will, Melissa needed the comfort and the security of Ben's embrace. She rose, found one of Ben's work shirts on the chair and slipped it over her shoulders, buttoning it just enough that it wouldn't fall off. She inhaled, loving the way Ben's scent enveloped her. Then she padded through the flat, looking for her lover.

The anticipation of finding him warmed her belly.

He sat in the dark lounge, in the same seat Will had occupied earlier. He didn't seem to notice her crossing the room, and when she sat beside him, he didn't acknowledge her presence. Surprised, she curled into his side, like she'd wanted to do in bed, and soaked up his body heat. "Hey, you."

Ben didn't answer.

There was an unexpected distance between them. An uncomfortable one. Almost as if Ben had pulled away from her emotionally.

She wasn't sure how to breach the chasm.

"Ben?"

"Mm?

"You okay?"

"I guess."

He guessed? "You wanna speak about it?"

Silence.

Mel hesitated, unsure what to do next. Ben was never this unresponsive with her. "Can't sleep?"

He shook his head. "Nope."

"It's lonely in your room without you."

Ben sighed. "I'm sorry, Mel. I'm just not up to making love at the moment."

She pulled away from him, stung. "I didn't come looking for you so you could fuck me. I came here because I missed you. The bed's empty without you."

. He didn't try to pull her back. "My mistake. I apologize."

Distant. He was so aloof. She wasn't quite sure how to deal with it. She stared at him, trying to make out his expression in the dark. It was impossible. "Would you like me to leave?" *God, say no. Please.* "I could go home."

Ben shook his head.

"You sure? It would give you some space." He may have said no, but he acted as though distance was exactly what he needed. Even so, her offer almost choked her. For weeks Ben had attempted to close the space between them, and now that he'd achieved that closure, now that Melissa wanted to be as close to him as possible, he seemed to have pulled away.

Fear and hurt stabbed at Melissa's belly.

What if he didn't want her anymore? What if he'd gotten all he could from her, shared her with his friend, and now thought it was time to move on? Time to make her into a memory, just like he had with that first woman he and Will had shared. The woman from the pub.

Or maybe she was just being paranoid. He hadn't exactly pushed her away or walked over to another seat. He just wasn't being as attentive as usual.

"I don't need space."

Okay, then what did he need? She didn't know, but she did know what she needed, and that was to show her gratitude to him. "I wanted to say thank you. For tonight." And for every other night he'd been with her. Fought for her.

"Tonight?"

"For what you did. Inviting Will to join us. It was..." She stumbled, seeking the right word. "It was amazing. Unbelievable. I've never experienced anything like that in my life."

Ben's entire body stiffened. His only response was to shift further away from her.

She tried not to let his coldness affect her. "It was incredibly generous of you. If the situation were reversed, I'm not sure I'd have been so willing to share." Scratch that. If Ben had been interested in another woman, Melissa would have been green with jealousy. She'd have wanted to claw the other woman's eyes out. And probably Ben's too.

Ben shrugged, his body still rigid. "Whatever, Mel."

Whatever?

That was his only response? What on earth was going on? Why was he acting like this? Hurt suffused though her, scraping at her heart. The warmth in her body seeped away.

She stood up. Perhaps being in separate rooms would be better. She wasn't ready to leave his flat. Not after everything that had happened between them, and not after she'd established how much she wanted him in her life. "I, er, I think I'll make some tea. Would you like some?" She could use a mug. Maybe a hot drink would warm her up. Maybe it would warm them both up—and the frigid atmosphere in the room too.

"No thanks."

Melissa waited another few minutes, but when Ben still made no attempt to talk, she gave up. She walked into the kitchen and put the kettle on. If after a drink he was still so aloof, she'd leave. She didn't want to feel alone at her lover's place. She could go home to experience that. At least there she'd have all her comforts around her.

She stretched as the kettle boiled, her muscles pleasantly stiff, her body thoroughly used—and pleasured. Ben was insane if he thought she'd sought him out to make love again.

She'd had two men inside her tonight. That was more than enough activity for any woman for one night, thank you very much.

But perhaps she deserved Ben's assumption. Hadn't she approached him to fulfill her sexual needs? Hadn't that been a pattern of behavior she'd developed over the past few weeks? Ben had every right to think that when she came looking for him all she expected was sex.

And yet tonight that was not what she wanted at all. She wanted to be held by him. Comforted. Soothed. She wanted to feel the reassurance of his affection for her. She wanted his love.

No, she craved it. Like an addict craved a fix.

Melissa sipped her tea alone at the kitchen table. The drink warmed her from the inside, but it didn't prevent the chills that sprang up on her skin as she made her way back into the lounge. Ben hadn't moved. Not an inch. And when she called his name, he didn't respond.

Pain lanced through her chest. "Please, Ben, I'm floundering here. I don't know what to say or how to act. Help me out. Tell what's going on. Tell me why you're acting like this."

"Acting like what?"

"Aloof. Distant. I-I'm getting a strong sense y-you don't want me here." That was it exactly.

Ben didn't want her there.

The knowledge hurt like hell. It crushed her ribs and squeezed her lungs. She hated how all the happiness that had settled inside her evaporated. Hated the insecurity his indifference wrought in her. Hated how uncertain she was— about herself and Ben's feelings for her and her very reasons for being here. She hated it all.

Unexpected tears filled her eyes, and she blinked them back, swallowing hard over the lump in her throat.

He snorted. "Not wanting you is hardly the issue."

She held out her hands in desperation. "Then what is?"

He didn't answer, merely shook his head.

"Talk to me. Please."

"Nothing to say."

"Nothing? After everything that's happened between us, you have nothing to say?"

Another shake of his head.

Melissa waited another moment or two, hoping against hope Ben would elaborate. He didn't. Nor did he look at her. She might as well have been invisible.

There was nothing left to say or do. She'd run out of options. Holding her shoulders back and her spine straight,

Melissa did her best to hide her misery. She collected her shoes and jacket from near the front door, and pulled them both on. Her garters and thigh-highs could stay on the floor in the bathroom. She had no need for them now.

"I-I'm going home." Why she'd announced her intentions, she had no idea. Ben obviously wasn't interested one way or the other.

Her heart sank, and the tears were back. She had to clear her throat before she could speak again. "Well, goodbye, then. Th-thank you again for earlier."

No response.

"I guess I'll see you at the office tomorrow." If he even wanted to see her. Judging from his behavior now, that seemed unlikely.

It was only when her hand touched the door handle that Ben finally spoke again. And when he did, he said the last thing she'd ever have expected.

"I shared Sienna with another man."

She spun around. "What did you say?"

"I fucked my fiancée at the same time as another man did." He gave an empty laugh. "Although, technically, she wasn't my fiancée anymore."

So, she'd been wrong. She wasn't the first woman he'd cared about that he'd shared with another man.

Every muscle in Melissa's body tensed. She so did not want to hear about Sienna right now. Not after everything she and Ben had been through together. Not after everything they'd done together. Everything they'd shared. Not after she'd realized she wanted his love and affection—more than she wanted her next breath.

But suddenly his distance made sense. He'd been thinking

about *her*. About Sienna. And Melissa wasn't Sienna. She never would be. Perhaps Ben was realizing that all too clearly. Perhaps he'd compared the two of them and found Melissa lacking.

"Is there a reason you're telling me this?"

He nodded. "So you'll understand."

"Understand what?"

"The hell I'm going through now."

Melissa stared at him, heartbroken and perplexed. "What hell?"

"The hell of knowing I shared you with another man."

She let her hand drop off the handle. "I really don't understand. Not at all." But she wanted to.

Her eyes were growing accustomed to the dimness, and she saw the grimace on his face. "I went after Sienna when she broke off the engagement. Wasn't ready to let her go. I followed her to a small island resort, thinking it would be the perfect place to convince her I was serious about us, serious about getting back together." He looked up at Melissa. "A tropical island. Romantic, no? A luxury hotel, balmy weather, sunset on the beach. The perfect place to heal a broken relationship, don't you think?"

She nodded. What else could she do? Beg him to stop speaking about his ex? Convince him he should be with her, not Sienna? Not likely. Ben was lost in his memories, and it didn't matter what Melissa said to him, she sensed she wouldn't reach him tonight.

"Sienna thought it was romantic too. Very romantic. So romantic, she met a guy there and fell in love with him."

"Ben..."

"I was arrogant, you know? Overconfident in myself and in

189

Sienna. I thought there was no way she'd refuse me. Seeing her with another bloke? It threw me. Made me jealous as hell. Made me even more arrogant. Made me think I was better than him. So I threw down the gauntlet. Challenged Sienna to sleep with both of us, at the same time, and then pick the man she liked more. I assumed she'd pick me. How could she not? We'd been together for eight years."

Melissa swallowed, unsure what to do next. Stand around, helpless, while Ben spoke, offer him comfort or leave. Hard choice, since Melissa didn't want to see Ben in pain, but she also didn't want to hear any more about Sienna. She didn't think her heart could take it. Besides, if his behavior over the last half an hour was anything to go by, he didn't want her anywhere near him.

"She didn't pick me." Ben shook his head. "She chose the other guy. Josh."

Melissa went to sit on the other couch. "You lost your own challenge."

"It hurt." He snorted, as though that might be the understatement of the century. "It fucking tore me in half. I thought I'd never recover."

Something about the way Ben said it made Melissa wonder what had hurt more: losing the challenge or losing the woman he loved?

"That's why I moved to Sydney. I had to get away from Newcastle, get away from my life there. It was so intertwined with Sienna's, I couldn't escape the pain, couldn't get away from the loss. Wherever I went, it surrounded me."

That same pain was so evident in his voice now, it made Melissa ache for him. Made her want to hold him in her arms, take the hurt away. She'd known hurt like that. She understood his pain. But Ben hadn't given any indication he wanted to be held. He'd only told her he wanted her to understand.

"There was no one after Sienna. Not for a long time. No one interested me. Until I met Will. And then he suggested a threesome." A long silence followed. "That was the night my dick found life again." His voice was hollow. "It wasn't an emotional thing, mind you. It was purely about sex. And fucking a woman while another man joined us."

"You sound as though you hated it." The first time he'd told her about it, he hadn't sounded this way at all. He'd portrayed it as fun, exciting and sexually stimulating.

"I did. Parts of it, anyway. Don't get me wrong. The sex was good. Always. In fact, until you walked into my office that night, it was the only thing that got me aroused. But I hated what it represented. Hated what it reminded me of."

His real love. "Your night with Sienna and her new guy?"

"My loss."

This time she had to know the answer. "Your loss of Sienna, or your loss of the challenge?"

"Both."

At least he was honest.

"Part of the reason I had so many threesomes with Will was the challenge. He never knew about it, but every time I fucked a woman with him, I silently challenged him. Waited to see who the woman would choose afterwards. Which one of us she preferred. Me or Will."

"You made them choose?" The idea horrified Melissa.

"No. Never. But I did watch them all very carefully afterwards. Took note of which one of us they'd gravitate towards."

"And?"

"Some gravitated to me, some to Will. Some left without a

backward glance, and some wanted both of us again."

"And this gave you pleasure?" Melissa tried to keep the horror from her voice.

"The sex gave me pleasure. The challenge afterwards? Not at all. But I found myself doing it time and time again. And now I understand why."

"Explain it to me." She wasn't understanding anything.

"It was my way of working through Sienna's rejection. My way of sorting it out in my head. I think I hoped that if enough women chose me over Will, my hurt pride would be healed. It wouldn't burn so much every time I thought about Sienna."

"And have you? Sorted it out, I mean? Is your pride healed? H-has the burn stopped?"

Ben nodded. "I thought so. In fact, after the first couple of months I'd stopped caring who the women chose. It no longer mattered. Until tonight."

Melissa pursed her lips, let Ben's words filter through to her consciousness. "Until I let you and Will fuck me at the same time." Her ribs contracted around her lungs, squeezing them, choking her. "I..." Breathing became impossible. "I was the challenge tonight."

Ben looked at her. He didn't deny it.

"You fucked me, with Will, knowing that after all was said and done it would be my turn to choose." Bile rose in her throat, and she fought the urge to be sick. "You set me up. Put me in a position to choose."

"I did." He agreed with such a dearth of emotion, Ben might have been discussing the weather.

"A-after everything we've been through together, everything we've done together, you..." She had to stop, take a breath. "You thought I might choose him?" Dear God. She'd lain in Ben's bed, not thirty minutes ago, marveling about how close she felt to him, how important he'd become in her life. How essential he was for her very breath. And he'd been sitting here, wondering who she'd choose. Him or Will.

"I...still think that." A wealth of pain accompanied his words.

Melissa stared at him, aghast. Horrified. Appalled. And crushed. He thought her capable of choosing his friend over him? Her? The woman who never let any man get close—except Ben?

Okay, so she'd made no promises to him, no pledges of love. In fact, she'd given him very little reason to believe she might choose him. But she'd changed. She was a different woman from the one who'd stalked into his office, stripped and demanded Ben fuck her. *He'd* changed her. Forced her to confront her life, view it differently. Forced her to let him into her heart.

No, she may not have openly said she'd changed, but Ben need only look at her, observe her behavior to know she was different. For heaven's sake, she was in his flat, spending the night. This from the woman who wouldn't let him walk her to her car just a few short weeks ago. Who'd balked when he'd phoned her at home.

How had he repaid that trust, that confidence she'd bestowed on him? Not by making her every fantasy a reality, like she'd originally thought. Not by wowing her with his generosity. Oh, no. He'd made her into a challenge. He'd given her the opportunity to choose another man. And to make matters worse, he believed she would choose that other man.

"You believe that if I walk out that door now, I'll go to him? To Will?" Surely he couldn't be that blind? That ridiculous?

"Yep. That's exactly what I believe."

Melissa's head reeled. He had that little faith in her. Ben, who'd always treated her with nothing but the utmost respect, who'd inspired her trust and confidence, believed the worst of her. Ben honestly thought she could walk away after a couple of hours spent naked with his friend.

The pain descended then. Like a million daggers, striking from all angles, cutting at her flesh, tearing at her insides.

"I let you in, Ben. I gave myself to you. I confided in you, told you my secrets. You know about my HSC. You know about Thomas. I shared things with you I've never shared with another soul." She had to gulp back the lump in her throat and blink several times to stop the tears from coming. "Physically, I gave you everything. Let you do things I've never let anyone else do. Trusted you to share me with another man for a night. And this is what you give me in return? This is the faith you have in me?"

Ben stared at the floor.

"You think I would choose another man over you? A man I barely know?"

Still he stared at the floor, but now he nodded while he stared.

She swallowed back the lump in her throat and attacked her cheeks with her hands, viciously wiping away tears that had leaked from her eyes. She wouldn't let Ben see her cry. *Would not.*

When her voice was steady enough that she trusted it to speak, she quietly said, "I thought you knew me better than that. Assumed you knew me better. "

His silence slayed her.

"Apparently you don't know me at all." Melissa rose to her feet. Wounded to the bone, she trudged back to the front door. "That's my cue to leave."

194

She hesitated, waited for the briefest of seconds, hoping against hope that he'd stop her from going.

He didn't.

She didn't hesitate this time. "Goodnight, Ben."

Ben didn't go to work the next day. Or the one after that. He didn't need to. He'd clocked so many extra hours these last few weeks, working late while waiting for Melissa, he could have taken three days' leave.

He needed the time to drown his sorrows in a bottle of scotch.

He'd planned the perfect evening for Melissa, given her everything she'd wanted, and in the process destroyed a piece of himself.

Instinct had told him from the beginning that he wasn't emotionally equipped to share her. He just didn't have it in him. He'd shared Sienna and lost her. If he lost Melissa he didn't think he'd survive.

But he'd done it. For her. He'd wanted her to enjoy everything she'd refused to enjoy up until now. Wanted her to see that life wasn't only about work and succeeding. It was about living too.

Ben polished off two bottles of scotch, and when his liquor cabinet failed to reveal another bottle, he opened a Chardonnay—one of the many he'd bought for Melissa.

She'd flourished under his and Will's attention. Blossomed. She'd loved every second of the threesome. Just as he'd intended. And if the truth be told, he'd enjoyed it almost as much. Sexually, it was an incredibly stimulating, exciting evening.

Emotionally it had flattened him. Crippled him. Terrified him.

He did in the wine and plowed into a second bottle.

He didn't want Melissa to choose. Never wanted the option to ever enter her head. He never wanted her to think that Will was a possibility.

But then he'd assumed Sienna would never think Josh was a possibility, and look how that had turned out.

Fuck. He'd done it again. Made the very mistake that had cursed his life. He'd shared the woman he loved with another man. And he hadn't done it purely for her pleasure. He'd done it to test her. To see if like Sienna, she'd also choose the other man. Or if possibly, just possibly, Melissa had developed feelings for Ben. Feelings like he felt for her. He'd done it to see if Melissa would choose him.

And he despised himself for putting her in that situation.

Ben would have opened a third bottle of wine, but he couldn't find one—even though he knew he'd bought at least a dozen bottles. He couldn't find the bottle opener either, which was odd, because he'd used it just a few minutes before, hadn't he? He also wasn't sure where his bedroom was. That blew his mind. He'd lived in the apartment for almost a year. Shouldn't he know by now?

He wandered around aimlessly until he found it.

Then he lay down on his bed—or maybe it was Melissa's bed. It kinda smelled like her. Like vanilla and cinnamon and sex—and slept the rest of the day, the entire night and well into the next morning.

He trudged into the office the next day, feeling just as unsettled and unrested as he had for the last two days. Very little had changed. The alcohol had done nothing but numb his senses—and leave him with the mother of all headaches. The pain, the heartache and the sense of utter failure on his part still remained. At least now he had a good idea of how Melissa had felt when she'd failed her HSC. How devastated she must have been.

Ben contemplated arming himself with a few caramel kisses and heading straight for Melissa's office. He decided against it. A couple of pastries were not going to heal the damage he had caused. They would not make everything better. Besides, he was too ashamed of his actions to face the woman he loved and had, in all likelihood, lost. Either to Will or to the stupidity of his own actions.

He knew he would face her. Just as soon as his thoughts were clear enough to work out what he wanted to say and the best way to say it. His mind, still pickled in alcohol, wasn't equipping him with appropriate words or ideas right now. He needed a plan. He needed to devise a way of apologizing to Melissa, of begging her to forgive him for his monumental screw-up and then of convincing her that for all his dumb-arse stupidity, she and he were meant to be together. She was never, ever, ever meant to be with Will.

Talking about whom... He tried not to look through his window, tried not to make eye contact with the man, but it was pretty damn hard when the view from his door led straight out the window and into the other man's office.

Ben turned his head, averting his gaze. But it was too late. He'd already seen something he couldn't quite believe he was seeing. Already comprehended something that made him long for those bottles of scotch he'd polished off a couple of days before.

Will wasn't alone.

Sitting in his office, right opposite him, was Melissa.

Chapter Fifteen

"I'm trying to make sense of it all." Melissa looked at Will, desperate to find answers she wasn't sure he could give.

"Come on, Mel. You're no fool. You understand what happened with the three of us."

She shook her head. "No. I don't. Not really. See, I'm not like you two, Will. I'm not out there sexually. I'm not used to experimenting and pushing my boundaries. This woman you've seen is not the regular me." She knew she was blushing. Not just because her cheeks burned, but because discussing this embarrassed her to no end. Humiliated her. She was attempting to find understanding and meaning from the third person in their ménage. The person with whom she shared no other bond save the kink he'd added to her nights.

Yes, she'd taken an instant liking to him, and the physical attraction between them had been strong, magnetic even. But that was where it ended. Neither was under any illusion the encounter would turn into anything more.

In fact, Will himself had made that pretty clear at Ben's apartment.

While Melissa still lay in a post-orgasmic haze, and Ben had disappeared into the bathroom to clean up and to find a washcloth for her, Will had dressed then leaned over and kissed her on her forehead. An affectionate kiss. A goodbye kiss.

"Thank you," he'd whispered. "For allowing me in tonight. For letting me share you with Ben just this once."

He hadn't waited for her to contradict him and talk about a

next time. He'd quite clearly told her there wouldn't be a next time, something that Melissa had assumed as well.

Though the evening had been fantastic, it was a one-off experience. She'd never considered it might be more. She'd never wanted more from Will. Ben gave her everything she needed.

Well, Ben *had* given her everything she needed, right up until the time he gave her the shock of her life.

Before that terrible moment, she'd kind of assumed that after the threesome, things would go back to normal between her and Ben. Or go back to being just the two of them, at any rate.

Boy, had she ever been wrong.

Nothing was the same. Nothing at all.

There was no "two of them" left in this whole sorry situation. Whatever had developed between Ben and her had been cut off cold. Ben hadn't acknowledged her since she'd left his place. Hadn't phoned, hadn't visited. He hadn't even come to work. Not a word had she heard from him, and his silence and absence ripped at her heart and her belly, leaving them lying in a thousand excruciating shreds.

Discussing all of this with Will was close to impossible for Melissa, opening up to someone else a foreign experience. Yes, she'd let Ben in, allowed him to see the real Melissa, but that had taken time and a truckload of trust. Will, well, with Will she was taking a chance. But something told her she could trust him. Perhaps it was the gentle and understanding yet passionate way he'd handled her while she'd been with him and Ben.

She was still surprised to find herself in his office. Surprised that he was the one she'd turned to. But somehow he seemed like the perfect person to seek advice from. He knew

Ben. He knew what had happened between Ben and her. He'd been there with them. And he was the man Ben had surreptitiously challenged. He was as much a part of this as they were. Well, not as much, since Mel liked Will but did not feel for him the depth of emotion she felt for Ben.

Melissa took a deep, fortifying breath. "I've never allowed a third person to watch me have sex. I've never had sex with two men. I chose the safe option every single time. Until now. Until Ben—and you."

Will smiled at her. An encouraging smile, as though sensing her trepidation in sharing all of this with him. "And why do you think that is? What is it about Ben, or about Ben and me, that brings out your wild side?"

Melissa stared at him, at a loss. She didn't have answers.

"Think about it, Mel. What made you step out of your comfort zone? What made it okay to experiment with us when you'd never experiment ordinarily?"

Okay, so maybe she did have answers. Maybe it was more a problem of not wanting to give away her secrets. But she'd come this far, had gotten up the courage to seek Will out. She couldn't pull back now. Besides, he was so warm and open and understanding, her instinct told her she could tell him anything. "I was bored," she admitted at length. "Bored and unsatisfied with my life."

"So spicing it up took away that boredom?"

She gave his question ample consideration. "It added excitement and entertainment and pleasure. Lots of pleasure."

"Leaving you satisfied?"

"Sexually satisfied."

"And emotionally?"

Melissa didn't answer.

"Are you still bored?"

Melissa's shoulders slumped. Misery overwhelmed her. And as it did, cloaking her in a blanket of gloom and depression, Melissa suddenly wanted to talk. Wanted to be honest with someone about her life, about how much she despised it. And since she was with Will, had come here anyway... "Can I be honest with you?"

He smiled gently at her. "I'd be disappointed if you weren't."

She dropped her head in her hands. "I hate my life, Will. Apart from Ben, I hate everything about it. I hate my job, I hate the choices I've made, I hate where I am." *Wow.* Okay. That *was* honest. Perhaps more honest than she'd been in the last twelve years. It was Ben's doing. He'd forced her to confront her life and her emotions too many times over the weeks. She could no longer deny her true feelings.

"And yet you continue to live your life every day without changing it?"

She did change it. Often. She sought to do better, sought to achieve more. But those changes didn't make her life essentially different. If anything they only got her more entrenched in living it. "I guess I do." She looked up at him.

"Why?"

"Because it's the life I chose to live. I can't just give it up."

He held up both hands in question. "Why not?"

Hah, he made it sound so simple. "Because one doesn't just throw one's ambition and goals aside. Doesn't give up because life gets boring." She'd spent years telling herself that. It was easy to say it to Will.

"So one is expected to continue living the same dull life forever, because that's what one expects of oneself?"

"Exactly." At least he understood.

"You know what, Mel?"

"What?"

"That's a crock of shit if ever I've heard one."

She jerked her head. "Pardon?"

His voice was still gentle, but now it was firm too. "If you're not happy with your life and with the choices you've made, move on. Make different choices. Do something else. There's no one shackling you down. You're your own free agent. Do what you want to do."

Okay, maybe he didn't understand after all. "That's a little simplistic, don't you think?"

"What's wrong with simple? You have complicated, and you're unhappy. Lose the complications. Make it simple."

"Is that what you tell your clients?" Melissa turned the conversation around, focusing it on him. "When they want to adopt a baby from overseas?"

Will laughed. "Never. There's nothing simple about intercountry adoption. But what I will say to my clients, every time, is, 'Make one hundred percent sure this is the path you want to take. Because it gets tough. It gets unbearable. You hit dead ends and curveballs. And there is no guarantee. Make sure this is the path you want to walk because once you start, you have to be committed to the process. The progression will be exhausting, discouraging and daunting. It will get you down, but the end point, which may be years down the line, will make it worthwhile.'" Will took a breath. "That's the only reason my clients stick it out and endure the hardship. Because the end goal is worth it. It's what they want more than anything else in life."

He tilted his head and looked at her questioningly. "Is that why you're so committed to your life, to your job? Because you know the end point you're striving for is ultimately what you want more than anything else?"

Success had always been what she'd wanted more than anything else. Success had always been her end goal. Or not failing again, at any rate. But hadn't she achieved success a hundred times over already? She'd passed her HSC the second time round, passed her tech courses—at the expense of her relationship with Thomas—passed her uni degrees, gotten the job she'd applied for and risen through the ranks of Preston Elks. What more could she achieve or do to prove she'd been successful? How much more successful did she have to be to silence the ongoing lament of her teenage self?

She wasn't that teenager anymore. She hadn't been for a long time. She'd left her behind, years ago, and changed into a different woman.

She had succeeded. Maybe she hadn't made partner yet, but everything else? Yes!

Ben had told her all of this, but at the time, she hadn't been ready to hear it. Now everything was different. Now she knew he was right.

All that success had never made her happy. And what she wanted now, was to be happy. At some stage, since being with Ben, her goals had changed. She no longer wanted success. Ultimately, she wanted happiness.

She blinked and finally answered Will's question with a shocked shake of her head. "Uh, I'm surprised to admit that the end point I've always worked towards isn't what I want. Not anymore."

Will didn't miss a beat, didn't stop to discuss her mammoth realization. He just picked up on her admission and went with it. "So change it. Change your goal. Work towards something you desperately want now. And before you try to argue with me or convince yourself otherwise, yes, it is just that simple."

Melissa stared, gobsmacked.

Maybe, just maybe, it was that simple. For long moments she sat motionless, letting the idea sink in. Letting it take root in her mind. Letting it grow. And finally, when she thought she might just have her mind wrapped around the idea, she gaped at him in wonder. "You know something, Will?"

"Nope, tell me."

"I think you're wonderful."

His eyes twinkled. "Not to mention sexy as hell and good-looking to boot."

"Not to mention that at all." She grinned at him. "You're the whole package, Will Granger." And that whole package had just opened Melissa's eyes to a whole new world.

"But I'm not Ben," he said quietly. Meaningfully.

She had the grace to blush. "But you're not Ben," she agreed.

"Do you love him?"

She bit her lip, considered her answer. And knew when she gave it, it was the absolute truth. It had been the truth for a very long time. Only now it was unavoidable. She no longer wished to deny it. "Very much."

Dear God.

She did. She loved him. So much she thought she might burst from it. The emotion filled her heart completely and threatened to overflow. She, Melissa no-time-for-romance-or-relationships Sparks, was head-over-heels, crazy, madly in love with Ben.

"Does he know?"

She bit her lower lip and shook her head. "No."

"Why not?"

"Because...I've never told him." But then she'd never realized she loved him. Not until Will asked.

Now she couldn't stop thinking about it, couldn't believe she'd been so daft, so ignorant as to not notice it before. Of course she was in love with Ben. She had been all along, even before anything had happened between them. These last few weeks had only cemented that love. Solidified it, in her mind.

"Ah. Okay." Will was silent for a minute, pensive. "He loves you too, you know."

Sudden sorrow shadowed her joy, making Melissa sigh. "I...I thought he did." He'd told her he did. "But now I'm no longer sure." Not after the other night. Not after he'd shared her with Will and then stepped back and waited for her to choose the other man.

Will stared at her pensively. "Let me tell you something. Benny Boy isn't the type to fall easily. Trust me. I've seen women shift mountains trying to get him to notice them, trying to get more than just a quickie with him. He's either been oblivious to their efforts or disinterested. But with you...he's neither. The man has fallen for you, Mel. He's fallen hard."

"H-how do you know that?" God, she wished she could believe him. Wished she had the faith Will did. But Ben's behavior after their threesome told her otherwise. He may have thought he loved her, but if that had been the God-given truth, he wouldn't have let her leave that night. He wouldn't have expected her to choose Will. Would he?

"Ben and I have shared women before. Lots of them. Not once has he ever shown possessiveness, ever given off a vibe that he'd rather be alone with any of them. Until you." Will pursed his lips. "He *hated* sharing you, did you know that?"

Melissa blinked in surprise. "You could tell?"

"Hell, yeah. He despised it, and in the moment, he despised

me. His expressions and his behavior told me the very act was eating him up inside."

The penny dropped. "Which is why you gave him an out. Told him we could stop."

Will nodded. "But he was determined to go through with it..." He hesitated, regarding her with wise eyes. "Because he thought it was what you wanted. He believed it would make you happy. And as he told me, he'd do anything you wanted, as long as it made you happy."

She gaped at him, speechless. He'd done it for her, to make her happy—even knowing how his threesome with Sienna had turned out. And if, as Will had said, Ben was still in love with her, he'd done it knowing he risked losing the second woman he loved.

Did that make him the biggest idiot on earth or the most generous lover a woman could ask for?

Possibly a bit of both.

"That bloke is gone for you, Mel. Bloody hook, line and sinker in love."

"He is?"

"He is."

Then that would make him the most generous lover a woman could ask for. Perhaps wrapped up with a little idiot.

Melissa jumped to her feet. "I have to speak to him."

"That'd be a good idea." Will stood too.

"I'm going, now. But first..."

"First?"

She stepped forward and hugged him tight. "Thank you, Will. For everything."

He hugged her back. "Trust me, beautiful, the pleasure was

all mine."

She could hear the smile in his voice. "That's where you're wrong, Mr. Granger. But I think, from now on, that blind on Ben's window will remain closed at night." It was time. If indeed Will was right, and Ben did love her, and she loved Ben, then it was time for just the two of them to be together. Alone.

He released her, and she stepped back.

"I've kind of been expecting that."

"You have?"

"You and Ben are good together. It's very clear. But now you need to be great together, and you don't need me there to complicate matters."

She smiled at him. "You really are wonderful, ya know?"

"I know." His answering smile was mischievous. Sexy. "And now..." Will hitched his thumbed at the window. "I think you'd better go back to your offices and deal with a very jealous colleague."

Melissa turned to look through the window. And there, in a complete reversal of roles, stood Ben—the man she loved—in the building next door, watching her and Will.

Chapter Sixteen

Ben hurt all over. The pain in his chest radiated outward until not one inch of his body remained unaffected. The ache was overwhelming. All encompassing. He couldn't see through it, couldn't get past it. He'd tried not to think about it. Tried to ignore it. Tried for hours. But the pain kept spreading, and the agony was unavoidable.

Melissa had been in Will's office.

Hell, fuck that. Melissa had been in Will's arms.

Nausea threatened to choke him.

He forced himself to take a steady breath and tried to quell the need to hit something—or somebody. Tried—

"Ben? Do you have a minute?"

Melissa.

She didn't wait for his response. Or maybe she did, but he spent so long formulating one, she finally gave up. "I have a document that needs proofreading. Do you mind?"

Yes, he fucking minded. He minded that she'd been in Will's office. He minded that she'd been in Will's arms. He fucking minded a lot. But then he'd been the one to drive her there, so he couldn't argue. He didn't have a leg to stand on.

Ashamed of himself, mortified right down to his bones, he wished he could take it all back. Wished he could change the way things had worked out between them. But what was done was done. There was no going back, only forward. And as soon as he was stable enough to move forward, he would. He'd go after Melissa with everything he had. Apologize to her. Profusely. Beg her forgiveness. And get her to see that Will was not the man for her. Ben was.

In the meantime, she was in his office, asking him to proof a document, and he was not at all prepared to see or face her. Couldn't she get Jerry, Sue or Pete to read through it? It'd be much easier on both of them that way.

Ben drew his shoulders back and, like Melissa had done a thousand times before, stepped into professional mode. He could not, would not let her see how put out he was. He'd proof her document like she asked. But if she thought for one minute he wasn't going to fight for her, wasn't going to win her back and make her love him like he loved her, she had another thing coming.

He wasn't going down without a fight. He'd fought for Sienna and lost. But then he'd been arrogant enough to think he hadn't stood a chance of losing. He wasn't that arrogant anymore.

He knew he stood every chance of losing Melissa. Probably already had. Will was a decent bloke, a real decent bloke. One of the best. But damn it, Ben loved her. Loved her! Against all odds he'd fallen in love with another woman. He wasn't about to let her walk off with the other man. Not this time. No matter how decent that man was.

Just as soon as she left his office, he would put his mind to it and come up with a foolproof plan. A plan Melissa would not be able to resist. A plan that would have Melissa back in his arms and back in his life for good. And this time, he would not challenge another man for her affections. He wouldn't be so fucking stupid. This time he would keep it between the two of them. Just him and Melissa.

He held out his hand. "Not at all. Bring it over." Hah. See?

Mel wasn't the only consummate professional in this office. He could act like one as well.

Although he couldn't help but wonder what Melissa would do if, instead of taking the document, he took her hand, hauled her in close and held her until she melted into him, became part of him.

Probably slap the crap out of him.

Ben expected several pages. Their contracts were never less than fifteen pages. But Melissa handed him just one. He looked at it in surprise. Then brought it close and began to read.

Two minutes later he read the entire thing again, and then once more to make sure he wasn't hallucinating.

"Are there any mistakes? Spelling errors? Addresses in the wrong place?" Melissa asked.

Ben shook his head. The letter was perfect. But that was irrelevant. "What the hell is this?"

"Exactly what it looks like. A letter of resignation."

"But...but it's signed by you. Written by you."

"Well, yes. Of course it is. It would be ridiculous if you wrote and signed my letter of resignation."

"You're leaving Preston Elks?" Impossible. Implausible.

"I am."

"Why?"

"Because I no longer wish to work here."

Full-blown panic slapped him across the face. Because of him? Because of what he'd done to her? Was he responsible for her complete change of mind?

"But you haven't made partner yet." Christ, if his challenge had interfered with her accomplishing something she'd worked towards her entire adult life, he would never forgive himself.

She nodded. "I know. Funny how that turned out. A month ago it was all I wanted, all I lived for. Now it holds no interest for me."

He jumped to his feet. "Mel, if this is about me, about what I did to you with Will, I'm sorry. So goddamned sorry. I never should have done it, never should have put you in a position to choose, never should have set up the challenge. It was a dumb-arsed, selfish thing to do, and I regret the day I ever involved you in my fucked-up psychological problems." His throat was raw. Talking hurt. "Just please, please, don't quit because of me. Don't ruin your life and everything you've worked so hard to achieve because I'm an idiot."

Mel listened with a raised eyebrow. "Well, I agree with one thing. You are an idiot. You should never have seen sex with me, you and Will as a challenge you had to win. Never have been such an idiot as to think I might even want to choose." She shrugged. "But even so, that challenge has nothing to do with my reasons for quitting."

"It doesn't?" Her answer confused him. It didn't let him off the hook, not by a long shot, but it did give him some measure of relief that she wasn't leaving because of their ménage. "Then why are you going?"

"Because you were right. It's ridiculous to live a life I hate. Ridiculous to work my arse off to earn a promotion I want only to prove to myself I can get it."

Ben rubbed a finger and thumb over his forehead, massaging the dull pain that had started a slow throb there. "I'm not going to lie. You're confusing the hell out me. You're quitting because you don't want to work here any longer?"

"I am. I hate investment banking. Have for a long time. But I'm only just learning that I don't have to remain in a job I hate just to prove I can succeed in it and reach the top. In fact, I no longer care if I succeed. It's not important anymore. It's not what I want."

"So your die-hard ambition to make partner? What, it's just...gone?" He snapped his fingers. "Like that?"

She gave a *humph.* "Funny, huh? But yep, there you have it. It's gone."

He stared at her in disbelief, unsure whether to celebrate with her or march her straight to the closest doctor's office out of fear she'd developed a serious mental illness.

"You're not messing around?" He held up the letter. "You honestly intend to give this to Preston?"

"Just as soon as I've popped it into this envelope."

Maybe he was the one hallucinating and this wasn't real. "And once you've handed it over? Then what? What do you plan on doing with your life?"

Melissa put a finger to her mouth, stared dreamily at the ceiling and smiled. "I don't have the faintest idea."

"You don't have another position lined up?"

"Nope."

"A meeting with a headhunter, perhaps?"

She shook her head.

"You have no idea, no plans?"

There it was. The dreamy expression again. "Not a single one."

Okay, now Ben was starting to worry. Big time. This was not Melissa. Not at all. This was a stranger standing before him. Granted, a happy, excited stranger, but a stranger nevertheless. The Melissa he knew would never give up her job in favor of...nothing.

"I don't get it. What happened?" He shoved a hand through

his hair, perplexed. "Three days ago you were determined to stay here and make partner. Determined to work towards your long-term goal. Today you're resigning. What changed?"

"*I* did. I realized that what once was important no longer is. I've started to see myself in a whole new light. Yes, I may once have been a failure, but I'm not anymore. I haven't been for a long time. But the thing is, remaining in a job I detest, living a life I don't want to live is in itself a failing. I'm failing me. I'm failing to make myself happy, and I can't do that anymore. I won't."

He gaped at her, astounded. "You're serious."

"Dead serious."

"This is what you want? You're sure?"

"Never been more sure in my life." She looked it. Looked resolute. But more than that, she looked happy, carefree and dreamy-eyed. She looked exactly the way he'd always wanted her to look: content within herself.

"What will you do, Mel? If you're not working here, where will you work?"

She grinned. "I have no idea. None. And I love that. Love that I don't have any direction in my life. Love that for once I can just settle back and appreciate life instead of letting it pass me by while I work." Melissa took a great big breath of air, inhaling as if for the first time ever she could appreciate its life-giving properties. "You know, I have you to thank for all of this. If you hadn't pushed me, hadn't made me open my eyes, I'd never have seen what I was doing to myself. I'd never have taken the time out to appreciate all life has to offer and I'd never have fallen in love. So yes, while you may be a complete arsehole for challenging Will for my affections, I forgive you. Because in the end it all worked out for the best."

Before Ben had a chance to process her words, before he

could make sense of them, Melissa marched over and kissed him on the cheek. A chaste, friendly kiss. "Thank you, Ben. For everything."

And then she was gone.

Ben had maybe a half a minute before comprehension slammed into him, leaving him winded.

What the fuck?

She'd fallen in love? And she had him to thank for it? He'd opened her eyes?

No way. No freaking way in hell was she walking away. Not now. Not ever.

If he'd opened her eyes to a different, happier way of life, if he'd helped her fall in love, then there was no way he was letting her go.

And it was too fucking bad if she'd fallen in love with Will. She was his. Ben's. They belonged together. They were explosive together. He would not lose her to another man. *Couldn't* lose her to another man. So help him God, if he had to get down on his knees and beg, he would. He'd do whatever it took to make Melissa see they were meant for each other.

With Sienna he'd formulated a long, involved plan in an effort to win her back, and then he'd been forced to change the plan to suit the circumstances that had greeted him on the island. He had no plan with Melissa. Had no time to prepare one. No time to look at his options and pick the best path of attack. He just knew that whatever happened from this moment on he could not lose her. He loved her too damned much to live without her.

Ben sprinted through his door, raced down the corridor

and took a right, heading straight for Preston's office. The exact place Melissa was headed, letter in hand.

He reached her a step away from Preston's receptionist, wrapped his arms around her waist from behind, and without a word of explanation to anyone, hauled her up and carried her into the corridor.

Melissa's yelp of surprise had people sticking their heads out of their doors all the way down the passage.

Ben didn't give a damn.

He set Melissa on her feet, flipped her around to face him and backed her against the wall, trapping her with his body, giving her no space to escape.

"Are you out of your mind?" he fumed. "What the hell are you thinking?"

Surprisingly, Melissa didn't try to escape. She didn't squirm or wriggle her way out of the prison he'd made by placing an arm on the wall on either side of her head. She didn't even ask him to release her and let her walk off with some dignity.

"I'm thinking I'm about to start living my life, and I can't wait. Although..." she looked first at his one arm and then at his other, "...it's pretty difficult to start anything from this position."

"So you're leaving? Just walking away without a backward glance?"

"Of course not. I'll give the company at least a month's notice. I'll stay longer if they need help training someone to take over my position. I might be excited about my new life, but I'm not going to shirk my responsibilities."

"From me," Ben growled. "I mean, you're just walking away from me without a backward glance?"

She scowled at him. "Hardly, Cowley. You have me trapped here. I can't go anywhere."

"You don't fucking get it, do you, Sparks?" Out of sheer frustration, Ben thwacked the wall with his hand. Hard. So hard his palm stung. "I *love* you. I am so goddamned, madly in love with you, I can't see straight." Ben's voice resonated through the offices, echoed in his own ears. "You're the first thing I think about in the morning and the last thing I imagine before I fall asleep. I dream about you. Every single night. I live to see you, at the office, at home, anywhere. I just need to see your face. Hold your body. Touch your skin. I need you, Mel. More than I need air. You can't walk away from me. You can't love someone else."

He gulped in a breath and almost choked on the emotion clogging his throat, so when he spoke again his voice was scratchy, and much, much softer. "I screwed up. I made you choose. And I'm sorry. So desperately, pathetically sorry for that. But I can't let you go. I can't let him have you, because you're mine. You were made for me, like I was made for you. We're two peas in a pod, sweetness. We're the same, you and I. We're meant to be together."

Melissa gaped at him, her mouth open, her hazel eyes enormous.

"Don't leave me, Mel." Now his voice was a rough whisper. The sheer intensity of his emotions sapped the strength to speak any louder. "Please, don't leave me because I so callously confused you with someone from my past. So stupidly got you mixed up in my head. I know who you are. I know you. And God help me, I love you more than I thought it was possible to love anyone ever again. Please, just don't leave. Don't choose Will, even if I put you into a position to do just that." He ran out of breath. Ran out of steam. "Please, don't walk away from me."

For long, long, long seconds, silence permeated the corridor, interspersed only by Ben's harsh breathing. The people who had popped their faces out of their doors now stood in suspended silence, listening, waiting. Even Melissa seemed frozen. She didn't move. Didn't breathe.

Ben's energy deserted him. His eyes closed in defeat, and his arms dropped to his sides. He couldn't keep her here, couldn't trap her in a relationship she didn't want. What kind of an idiot was he, thinking he could?

"I'm quitting my job, Cowley," Melissa said, forcing Ben to open his eyes and look at her. "That's all. I'm leaving work. Changing my lifestyle. I'm not walking away from you. I'm not choosing someone else. That choice was never an option for me. It was one you made up inside that thick head of yours." She clunked him on his forehead with her knuckles as if to prove her point. "I love you too. I'm stupidly in love with you. Wholly and completely in love with you. It just took me a while to realize it."

It was Ben's turn to gape. Ben's turn to stare at her with enormous eyes, while his heart sat in his throat.

"Oh, come on. You didn't honestly think that after everything you and I have been through together, I could up and fall in love with another man, did you?"

"I didn't think at all, Mel. That was my whole problem. I just acted on instinct, assuming you'd respond the same way Sienna did."

Melissa bristled. She snarled and got in Ben's face, speaking in a voice so low and so gruff, there was no way anyone else could hear her. "Okay, now you listen up, and you listen good. I'm not her. I'm not Sienna. I don't look like her, I don't think like her, and I am tired of hearing you refer to her all the time. If you and I are going to work, if we're going to stand a chance, you have to give her up. You have to forget about Sienna, because I refuse to spend the rest of my life competing with her for your affections."

Ben shook his head and gave a helpless laugh. "Sweetness, I gave her up the first time I held you in my arms. Whatever I once felt for her slipped into the past. What I never let go of were the mistakes I made with her. They haunted me, enough that I made the same mistakes with you. The difference is, I'm not letting those mistakes go unacknowledged. I'm not letting them ruin us. I can't give you up. I can live without Sienna. I can't live without you."

"Oh, Cowley." Melissa sighed. "The only mistake you made was thinking I might be dumb enough to want to choose someone else. Everything else you did, you did to make me happy. I understand that. And I forgive you. Just swear that you'll never, ever put me in that position again."

"I swear that from now on I'll only ever put you in a position you want to be in, Mel. But you'll never have the chance to choose again, because I don't believe I can ever share you again. Not with anyone."

"I'm okay with that," Mel whispered.

"You are?"

She nodded. "I am."

And then she smiled. The very smile that lit up his office. Now it lit up his life. He smiled back, and his heart filled with an intense joy the likes of which he hadn't felt for a very long time. No, correction, the likes of which he'd never felt before.

"Oh, for God's sake," a voice called down the passage. "Just kiss her already."

"Yeah." Another voice. "Stop buggering around and do it."

A chorus of "Kiss her!" followed that.

Ben grinned at her. "What do you say, sweetness? You wanna kiss me in front of the entire staff of Preston Elks?"

Melissa grinned right back at him. "There is nothing I'd like more."

And right there, in the corridor of Preston Elks, they kissed. On the mouth, with tongue, for everyone to see.

About the Author

Apart from her family and friends, Jess Dee loves two things: romance and food. Is it any wonder she specializes in dee-liciously sexy romance? Jess loves hearing from readers. You can email her at jess@jessdee.com or find her at www.jessdee.com.

Adolescent fantasies can grow into very adult realities.

Island Idyll

© 2011 Jess Dee

Bandicoot Cove, Book 4

Sienna James has come to Bandicoot Cove to mourn the end of her eight-year relationship with Ben Cowley. The last person she expects to meet is the star of every one of her high school fantasies.

Joshua Lye is not only as appealing as he was in high school, he reveals she was the main feature in his adolescent wet dreams. As kids they never got it together. But they're adults now, and there's nothing keeping them apart.

When Ben arrives at the resort determined to win Sienna back, finding another man in her bed kind of throws a spanner in the works. But he isn't deterred. Rather than admit defeat, he comes up with an alternative plan: Let Sienna sleep with both men—at the same time. Then she can make an informed decision as to which man she wants.

Sienna shouldn't want to go through with this shockingly sexy plan, but she does. Desperately. Except after the sexual storm passes, she could have it all...or be left holding an empty heart.

Warning: Contains a suggestion beyond risqué, a solution beyond orgasmic, and two men who know how to play dirty. Really, really dirty.

Available now in ebook from Samhain Publishing.

He's got one shot. Better make it naughty...

Just One Night
© *2012 Chloe Cole*

Micah's new living arrangement with her best friend is quickly becoming unbearable. Not because Tomas isn't a good roommate. When they're alone, he shows her his sweet, loyal side. It's just that he shows the rest of his parts to half the women in town. If she can't scrape together the money for her own place soon, witnessing the aftermath of his late-night carousing is going to break her heart.

Then again, if it's going to break anyway, maybe she should just go ahead and make a move on the man she's loved since high school. And risk his rejection a second time.

It hasn't been easy for Tomas to share space with the one damsel he can't bear to see in distress. To have her within easy reach has been torture. His foster mother's words echo in his head: a classy girl like Micah deserves more than the likes of him. But lately Micah's been rattling his cage. If she does it one more time, she'd better be ready for the animal she awakens.

Unfortunately for him, Micah's hot little hands are already wrapped around the bars...

Warning: Contains a Latin bad boy with twelve years worth of fantasies to get out of his system, and his goody-two-shoes best friend who learns that her inner bad girl likes handcuffs and spankings. Beware. This book could cause a riot since there's only one Tomas to go around.

Available now in ebook from Samhain Publishing.

www.samhainpublishing.com

Green for the planet.
Great for your wallet.

It's all about the story...

Romance

HORROR

Retro ROMANCE

www.samhainpublishing.com

CPSIA information can be obtained at www.ICGtesting.com
Printed in the USA
LVOW081531070313

323211LV00010B/1233/P